FIRE STORM

An Angela Masters Detective Novel

By Mike Worley

ISBN 978-0-9960118-2-2
Published in the United States by Mike Worley Books

Dedication
To my wife and principal editor, Nancy, without whose love
and support this project would not have been possible.

Chapter 1

2:14 a.m. — June 29, 1985. No one knew how the fire started. It had flared a day earlier, high up on the Mayacamas Mountains ridge above Santa Rosa, California. What everyone did know, thanks to around-the-clock local news coverage, was that the previous winter had been extremely mild. Now the trees and underbrush of Sonoma County were tinder-dry.

The fire marched relentlessly to the west and crossed Wallace Road. The prevailing westerly winds were maddeningly light and the fire just sucked the wind into itself. Building speed, the wind fueled the raging blaze rather than slowing its headlong march. It would soon threaten the half-million-dollar homes in the exclusive areas off the Fountaingrove Parkway. Santa Rosa's citizens turned out by the hundreds to witness the inferno. The parkway and surrounding streets were choked with cars, some haphazardly abandoned in traffic lanes as gawkers sprinted to see the dancing, roaring orange monster for themselves.

"I'm bringing in extra officers on overtime to help with crowd and traffic control," John Porter, the patrol division captain, told Chief Hathaway earlier in the evening. "It's nuts up here. At one point so many gawkers had abandoned their cars to run to see the fire that the cars blocked a fire truck from getting to the scene. After about five minutes, the truck captain just ordered his driver to push the civilians' cars out of the way.

"So, I've ordered the regular patrols to run light in the rest of the city and I'm only augmenting traffic control to let the fire department do their job. The battalion chief told me it's turned into a Black Fire — heavy smoke with high winds that the fire itself is generating."

* * *

On the other side of the city, in a quiet neighborhood off Sebastopol Road, Alan Douglas felt exhausted but wide awake at the same time. The banquet manager for the Hilton Hotel in downtown Santa Rosa hadn't gotten home until nearly 1:30 a.m. A pre-Fourth of July party at the hotel had gone longer than planned and Alan had decided to stay to supervise the clean-up after the guests finally left.

His wife and two young sons were in bed upstairs and Alan didn't want to disturb them. Besides, he was still keyed up and was sure he wouldn't sleep well. But as he stretched out on the couch in the living room, he dropped off in less than ten minutes.

His rest was short-lived. The loud banging on the front door, accompanied by panicked, high-pitched screams, brought him to his senses almost immediately.

"No, no, *please*! Noooo."

The moment his feet hit the carpet, the screaming seemed to move away from his threshold. He turned on the porch light and cautiously peered through the peep-hole in the door, but saw no one. Still, what he had heard disturbed him.

* * *

"Santa Rosa 9-1-1. What is your emergency?"

"My name is Alan Douglas. Someone was just banging on my door screaming for help. It sounded like a woman, but could have been a man with a high-pitched voice. I'm not sure."

"Is the person still there now?"

"I don't think so. I looked out the peephole and didn't see anyone. Can you send someone out right away?"

"I'll pass the information on to the patrol car in your area and have the officers check it out, sir. It might be a few minutes. We're pretty busy because of the fire over on the hills, you know."

"Just tell them to hurry."

* * *

"What was that, Jackie?" another dispatcher asked when the call was ended.

"Sounds to me like some kid playing a prank. I'll let the area car know to do a drive-by but it doesn't sound like anything big."

"Good," the other dispatcher said. "I'm dreading if something major happens. We are so short-handed on patrol across the city and the officers up on Fountaingrove probably couldn't get out of there if they tried, what with all the looky-loos blocking the roads."

As if in response, the emergency phone line rang.

"Santa Rosa 9-1-1. What is your emergency?" Jackie answered.

"Someone just robbed my store!" the caller said, his voice punctuated by labored breathing.

Jackie sat up in her chair, her senses on full alert. "What is your location, sir?" The caller gave the name of a convenience store on the near southwest side of the city.

3

"Can you give me a description of the robber?"

"White. He was in his mid-twenties, I think. He was wearing a gray hooded sweatshirt, which I thought was strange in this heat. But he pulled a gun on me and emptied the cash register before I could even think about it. He ran out the door headed west."

"Did you see a car?"

"No, not in the parking lot anyway. He ran off on foot."

"OK, sir. Lock your store. Patrol cars and a detective will be there very soon."

The pounding on Alan Douglas's door was forgotten in the intensity of the moment.

* * *

Douglas sat back on his living room couch. He could no longer hear the screams and his weariness soon caught up with him.

Five hours later, his wife came downstairs and woke him. "Alan, why didn't you come to bed last night?"

"It was late and I didn't want to bother you and the ... I need to check something."

"What is it?"

"Last night, someone was banging on the door, late, like at 2:30. I looked out the peep-hole but didn't see anything. I called the cops to check it out, but I want to be sure no one vandalized our house."

Douglas cracked open his front door and peeked out. Seeing nothing out of place, he opened the door wider and started to step out on the porch, when his wife screamed. She was staring, wide eyed, at the front door.

Douglas turned and jumped back gasping. He reached for the phone and again pressed the buttons for the emergency phone number, staring open-mouthed at the door.

On the gloss finish of the wood was a handprint, cast in blood.

Chapter 2

8:20 a.m. – June 29. Angela Masters was sleeping late, an unusual activity for her. Five foot ten, with long blonde hair, she was trim and athletic. Angi, as she was known, looked every inch the star athlete she once had been. A Santa Rosa native, she was a straight 'A' student and stand-out volleyball player, with a competitive spirit born of tremendous sorrow in her life.

Angi attended Cal State – Northridge on a volleyball scholarship. She was an outstanding student and a four-year starter as the setter on the Matadors volleyball team.

She graduated with honors and a degree in business administration. At 22, she returned home to Santa Rosa, but with no intention of making a career in the business world. Angi's uncle was a Sonoma County deputy sheriff.

She grew up listening to his stories of manhunts and arresting felons. That, and tragedy in her own life, made police service the only logical choice for her. She took the entrance test and was hired as a Santa Rosa city police officer at age 23.

Now, at 37, she was one of four detectives assigned to the violent crimes unit, where she was known as a workaholic, a sobriquet she wore with honor. Her days were spent tracking robbers, rapists, and murderers. It was work she loved and it gave her satisfaction like little else in her life.

But this was not her weekend to be on-call. She and Julie Phelps, a fellow violent crimes detective, were planning a trip to the Napa Valley wine country, across the mountains to the east. The Napa Valley was one place that gave Masters a sense of peace. She loved going there, although her trips were usually taken alone.

But for this weekend, Phelps had asked Angi to show her around the valley for a 'girls day out.' Masters and Phelps didn't often socialize. Julie was married and the two had little in common beyond work. But today, they would spend the day as tourist girlfriends. Angi was looking forward to showing her colleague around the wineries. That was until the phone rang.

"Sorry, Angi, but I have a call for you," the voice of Sergeant Michael Garrison said.

"I thought Devon was on-call this weekend," she muttered, half-protesting. But she was also intrigued to know what horrendous crime needed her attention.

"He's already out on an armed robbery from earlier this morning, and this one can't wait. I know it messes up your Saturday, but ..."

"Hey, the job comes first. Not a problem, Mike. What you got?"

"Suspicious circumstances is all we have right now, but it doesn't sound good. Hagen is the primary patrol officer on-scene."

Angi had mixed feelings. Certainly the Napa trip would have been fun, but this was a case — a test of her wits against some unknown perpetrator. She quickly called Julie and apologized for canceling their plans. She was dressed and out the door within ten minutes.

* * *

Twenty minutes later, Angi guided her tan Chevy Caprice to the curb, a block away from a knot of uniformed police officers. As she left her car, the group broke up and all officers but one fanned out in every direction. The remaining policeman, Senior Officer Jared Hagen, spotted Angi and walked to meet her.

"What's doing, Jared?" she asked.

"We don't know for sure yet," Hagen said. "The reporting party, a guy named Alan Douglas, called in last night and claimed to have heard someone banging on his front door and screaming for help. Dispatch never sent anyone and didn't even notify the area car."

"Seems a little odd. Why not?"

"Well, I guess they were running pretty short on regular patrol last night because of the fire. A lot of units were up there directing traffic. Anyway, the dispatcher apparently thought it was probably some kid pulling a prank on Douglas. She meant to give the area car a heads-up but it somehow slipped her mind. I guess right after that was when the 211 occurred that Anderson is out on."

"Yeah, Garrison told me he was on an armed robbery call. Mike also said this Douglas guy is pretty upset. Didn't anyone explain to him what happened?

"Yes, when the guy heard the screaming a little after two, he peeked out but didn't see anyone, so he just called it in as a suspicious circumstance. Then this morning, he went to look outside because he was concerned about possible vandalism. That's when he saw the bloody handprint on his door. He's pissed because he thinks the police should have responded and found that first."

"Well, I can't say I blame him. I wouldn't want to find a bloody handprint on any door in my neighborhood, let alone on my own door. So he didn't see anything, or anyone, that would help us figure out what was going on?"

Hagen shook his head.

"OK. Let's go ahead and get a written statement from him. In the meantime, have your guys found anything else?"

"Unfortunately, yes. And in part, that's also why Douglas is upset. There's a lot more blood around the neighborhood."

"How much more?"

"A lot! We found blood drops and even small pools of it in at least five front yards."

Angi could see at least ten or twelve orange traffic cones in various places within a half block of the Douglas house.

"I had the other guys cone the places where we found blood drops or pools. There's also another bloody handprint on a window on that house across the street — the one where Toni Burton is standing. I posted her to make sure that print doesn't get smudged before the lab can get here."

At that moment, a white van emblazoned with *Santa Rosa Police Mobile Crime Lab* in dark blue letters pulled to the curb. Angi was glad to see that Kim Williams was driving. This case was shaping up as one that would need the best lab technician available.

Chapter 3

9:05 a.m. — June 29. Kimberly Amber Williams fit that description perfectly. The transplant from the Boston area spoke with an accent that was sometimes difficult for the Californians to understand. Her work, however, was as meticulous and clear as any detective could hope for. Now, at only 31 years old, she was the acting supervisor of the police crime lab.

"Kim, I'm glad you're here," Angi said as the two women met near one of the blood pools. "Sounds like we've got a real mess, as a crime scene and also from a PR perspective." Angi briefed the lab boss on what she had learned from Hagen and Garrison.

"Yeah, Mike told me a little bit about it when he called me out. I've also alerted Aaron and he should be here soon. But I'm just a lab rat. Detectives like you get to handle the *pee-ahh* stuff," she said, grinning.

"Thanks for reminding me. I'd suggest you start with that house where Toni is standing. Jared tells me that there's a bloody handprint on the glass that's still showing ridge detail. Maybe that will lead us to our victim at least."

"You got it, *Bahhss*."

* * *

"Hi, Toni. What do you have?" Kim asked as she approached the uniformed officer.

"The woman who lives here came out this morning when she saw all the commotion of the officers responding to the 9-1-1 call. After she talked to a few neighbors, she was going back inside when she noticed a bloody handprint on her front window. You can see it there in the lower left corner of the glass."

Kim nodded.

"When she saw it, she screamed. I happened to be standing not far away and responded. After she pointed it out to me, I notified Hagen and then we just sealed the area off to wait for you and Angi."

"Has anyone taken a look at the print up close?"

"No. We couldn't get back there without disturbing the bushes under the window and I was afraid there might be some other evidence in or on the bushes. I got close enough to see that it looks like there might be some ridge detail on the print but that was about it."

"Good thinking, Toni. Thanks."

Kim returned to her van. She was unloading her scene processing kit when a beat-up gray Mazda screeched to a stop directly behind the vehicle.

"I got here as quick as I could, Kim. I was ... "

"It's okay, Aaron. I'm just about to process a print that someone, maybe our victim, left in blood on a window."

"OK! What do you want me to do?" the young assistant lab tech asked.

"Well, first of all. Take a breath. We have plenty of time. It's not that hot yet, and patrol has the scene locked down."

Aaron McDonald smiled faintly and nodded.

"See those traffic cones? Those are all blood drop locations. Would you take care of processing those?"

"Sure thing, Kim."

"And I'll be working on the bloody print on the window."

* * *

Before approaching the window, Kim took a series of photographs of the area in front of the house. The photographs depicted increased detail as she moved closer to the location of the handprint. They would provide a visual journal of the scene, should it later be needed in court.

Interesting that the plants are positioned that way, she thought as she snapped the scene overview pictures. The plants, boxwoods, were the most common plant used for hedges, but these were planted further apart. And instead of the usual 'flat-top' pruning of the bushes, these are shaped almost like pears — bulbous at the bottom and tapering to a near point at the top.

There was some kind of disturbance there, though. Maybe a fight. Two of the bushes closest to the handprint showed signs of breakage, as though someone had either fallen into them or had otherwise struck them with considerable force.

As Kim got closer, she could see that there was more to the scene than just a bloody handprint. The amount of blood visible was a strong indicator that at least one person who had been in these bushes was badly wounded. She also noted that some of the branches weren't broken but were cut. The fresh boughs lay on the ground, painted with a patina of drying blood.

Kim turned her attention to the handprint. It was a depiction of a full hand, the right hand of someone whose palm had been thoroughly inked. It reminded her of the prints she had seen small children make in kindergarten. They dipped their little hands in smooth tempura paint and placed them carefully on a piece of construction paper — a gift for their parents. But the paint in this case was blood, probably human blood.

She took a few more photographs of the handprint, and ...

"Anything useful, Kim?" The voice of Officer Burton caused her to jump and nearly drop the camera. "Oh, Kim, I'm sorry. The

Sarge wants to cut me loose to go back on patrol but told me to check with you before I leave."

"It's OK, Toni. I was just concentrating I guess. And in answer to your question, yes. The blood had dried a little on the person's hand before this print was made. When she touched the glass, it was almost like leaving a layer of clay on the window. The ridge detail of the finger- and palm-prints is clearly visible. I'm saying 'she' because the handprint looks too small to be a man's. If this person is in the system, we'll have an ID before long."

As she spoke, Kim turned to her right and the corner of her eye caught something in the top branches of a boxwood near the center of the large picture window. "Toni, before you go, could you have Angi come over here?"

"Kim, Toni said you needed to see me right away. Did you get a good print from the window?" Masters said as she approached. Kim broke her concentration from the bush.

"Yeah, Angi, but we might not need it. Over here in this bush, there's a human hand, completely severed at the wrist."

Chapter 4

9:30 a.m. — June 29. Angi walked to the command post van. Sergeant Ted Simmons had assumed command of the scene and was coordinating the canvass efforts from there.

Her mind was reeling. *What the hell happened here?*, she thought as scenarios flipped through her mind like a rolodex of possibilities. She felt a shiver as she pictured a person, savagely wounded and desperate for help, pounding on doors in the neighborhood.

"Hey, Sarge," Angi said as she entered the van. "What's the status on the fire?"

"The fire department and the California Department of Forestry have made some progress in knocking it down. It's still threatening some homes but it looks like the air tankers they brought in last night are having an effect. Anything else you need patrol to do here?"

"Yeah. Kim just found a severed hand in the bushes of the house where we spotted the print on the window."

"No, shit! A severed hand? This one is getting weirder by the minute."

"Can we get the word out to the guys to be alert for any other body parts? And if we can get a few more officers here, that would be great. This isn't looking good for the victim."

"You got it. I'll get the info out to everyone now. And the good news is that since they're getting the fire under control, the crowds up on Fountaingrove have diminished. I'll check with the captain to see if we can divert some of those on overtime down here to help with the canvass. Sounds like this will be a real shit storm."

"Do it, Ted," Captain Porter said as he stepped into the van. "I heard a little of what Angi told you and I agree. This merits overtime just as much as crowd control at the fire. I'll brief the chief."

"Thanks, Captain," Angi said. "To what do we owe the pleasure?"

"I just left the fire scene and I wanted to see what was going on here. Sergeant Garrison is on his way here as well to get you any additional investigative resources you need."

"Thanks. I think we'll need it. At first, I was okay with just getting a statement from Douglas, the witness from last night. But now, I really need to talk to him, but I'm afraid he might be hostile unless we can show him that we didn't drop the ball on his call."

"Well, we did," Porter said. "Not deliberately, but we did. I think the dispatcher was trying to use good judgment on assessing his call, but she blew it when she didn't at least give the area unit a heads-up to do a drive-by. The 211 call certainly was a factor, but we all know we have to stay focused on the big picture."

* * *

"OK, I understand. I guess someone pounding on a door isn't a big deal in the whole scheme of things," Douglas said as he sat in his living room with Porter and Masters.

"We screwed up on this, Mr. Douglas, and both Captain Porter and I apologize for that. We still should have had the area car check for any trouble. But I really need your help now," Masters said.

"Yeah, I heard from one of the officers' portable radios that you found somebody's severed hand across the street. Was it from the person who was banging on my door?"

Damn, Porter thought. *I absolutely have to get earpieces for the officers' portable radios. Sure that was on the TAC channel so it wasn't monitored by the media, but what if it had been a suspect that overheard a radio transmission?*

"We don't know, Mr. Douglas. The lab technicians are working on that right now," Angi said. "But I'm pretty certain of one thing. Whoever was injured that badly probably didn't leave this area alone, and it's possible the whole thing started somewhere around here.

"Is there anyone in the neighborhood that you would consider suspicious? Maybe someone who is fairly new to the neighborhood? Maybe keeps to themselves and doesn't socialize with their neighbors?"

"Detective, you are exactly describing the house four doors down the street from here. It's a rental now. The people who own the house lived in it for years — long before we moved into the neighborhood — but they're older and they moved to Arizona two or three years ago. They have a property management company that kind of looks after the house and handles the rental.

"The guy who lives there now moved in maybe a month or so ago. He always keeps the curtains closed and doesn't seem to have a regular job. At least, from what I've heard, he doesn't come and go from the house at any regular time like he was going to work. But there's never any other cars there either, like I've heard you see if there's drug dealing going on."

At that moment, Douglas's wife walked into the living room. "Can I get water or anything for anyone?"

"No, thank you, ma'am," Porter said.

"Sonja, this is Captain Porter and Detective Masters. My wife, Sonja."

"Nice to meet you, ma'am," Angi said. "Your husband was just telling us about a house down the street where the guy is kind of reclusive."

"The Kalder's house, Sonja," Douglas said.

"Oh, yes," Mrs. Douglas said. "Very strange guy."

"Have you met him, ma'am?" Angi asked.

"No, but I saw him once. A week or so ago, I was visiting with Kelly — Kelly Hammond, who lives next door to that house — and the guy came out. I said 'hello' to him, but he just put his head down and walked away. Kelly told me that's the way he acts every time she's tried to speak to him. She said she thought there's been a woman there too, but not all the time."

"What did the guy look like?"

"He was a small man, maybe five-foot-eight or nine. He was wearing regular work clothes, jeans and a t-shirt when I saw him. But the thing that stood out to me was his big bushy beard. It was dark and curly and the whiskers were probably four or five inches long. He had long curly hair, too, down to his shoulders."

"Do you happen to know the guy's name?"

Sonja shook her head.

"No," Douglas said. "But I think the property management company is Detwiler. They're someplace downtown."

"Thanks. I think that's all the questions I have for now. I really appreciate your willingness to come forward," Angi said.

"You're welcome, Detective. I just can't believe something like this happened in our neighborhood."

* * *

"I think I'll wander down and take a look at that house, Captain," Angi said when the officers were outside.

"OK, Angi. I'll have a couple of the uniforms go with you."

"Thanks, Boss. But I'll let you know if I need anything. I'd like them to continue with the canvass for now."

The house which Douglas had indicated stood apart visually from the rest of the neighborhood. It was an old Victorian-style structure which had once been white, but peeling paint left most of the clapboard siding looking a wintery gray. The house was in stark contrast to the more modern houses of most of the residents, single story structures with low pitched roofs.

The lawn of the Victorian, just small tufts of grass punctuated by bare earth and yellowed weeds, hadn't been mowed in the perceptible past.

I hope the owner isn't paying this property management company very much, Angi thought.

The front door was as weathered as the siding. Two wires hung from a hole in the doorframe, the remnants of a long gone doorbell button. Angi knocked forcefully on the front door, but got no answer. The windows immediately adjacent to the door were covered with heavy cloth. *I can't see shit in there, and who covers their windows with canvas?*

Without a search warrant or exigent circumstances, Angi had no authority to move to other areas of the property. And she didn't have enough information to support a search warrant. As yet, there was no link between the bloody scenes down the street and the resident of the dilapidated house, regardless of any strange behavior.

But there was more than one way to gain information. The detective walked to the house next door to the suspicious house, the residence that Mrs. Douglas had identified as belonging to the woman named Kelly Hammond.

"Ms. Hammond, I'm Detective Angela Masters. I'm investigating a possible crime down near the Douglas house and I'd like your help."

"The Douglas house? Are Sonja and Alan okay?"

"Yes, ma'am, they're fine although a little shaken up. But Mrs. Douglas told me about some strange dealings you might have had with the man in the house next door. I'm wondering if it would be okay with you if I take a look at that house from your back yard."

"Sure. I mean, that's ok with me, but why can't you just walk into their back yard?"

"I can't legally go on to their property except to a place that's normally open to the public, like the front door. That is unless I have their permission, a search warrant, or what's called exigent circumstances. If I see something that leads me to believe there might be criminal activity from a place I'm legally allowed to be, then I can go ahead and go to the house. If you allow me to go into your back yard, then I would be looking at the back of the house from a place that satisfies the law."

"Then, by all means, come in. If anybody around here would be involved in something shady, it would be that character."

Chapter 5

9:55 a.m. — June 29. Kim took eighteen or twenty photographs of the human hand in the boxwood bush from every angle she could think of. She then carefully lifted the severed appendage from the bush between her latex-gloved thumb and forefinger.

Good, she thought, *it hasn't significantly desiccated yet.* The hand still retained enough moisture to produce a usable fingerprint. She pulled an aluminum spoon from her go-bag and inserted a print square. The spoon was actually a metal trough about three inches long. It allowed her to take a fingerprint impression without actually 'rolling' the finger. Rather than a standard fingerprint card, the spoon was designed to hold a self-adhesive square of paper, the exact size of a finger square on a fingerprint card.

Small tabs on the spoon held the square in place as Kim carefully inked a finger of the severed hand and then pressed it into the spoon. She then removed the protective paper from the back of the square and gently pasted it over the appropriate box on a fingerprint card. She repeated the process for each finger and the thumb.

When she was satisfied that she had a usable set of fingerprints from the hand, she slid the appendage into a plastic zip bag and sealed it. She wanted to preserve the moisture content for the present, although the hand would later be frozen for storage.

The lab tech then turned her attention to the bloody hand print on the picture window. Although it seemed likely that the handprint was made by the severed hand in the bushes, Kim could not rely on that assumption. Every possibility had to be covered in the evidence gathering process.

She also collected samples of blood from several spots around the window. As she was finishing her evidence-gathering, Aaron McDonald walked up.

"It certainly doesn't look good for our victim, or victims," Kim said.

* * *

Angi followed Kelly Hammond through her house to the back yard.

"Is it okay if I go with you?" Kelly asked.

"Of course." Angi would have preferred that the woman not accompany her, but it was Hammond's own back yard and Angi was there with her permission. She was in no position to tell Hammond she could not follow.

The two women walked a few feet into the yard and turned toward the fence separating Hammond's yard from the back of the rental property. Suddenly, Hammond put her hand to her mouth and stifled a scream.

Angi saw it at the same time. The back door of the rental house was covered with blood.

"Let's go back inside, Ms. Hammond. We don't need to see any more of this. This is all I need right now but I will want to talk to you later about this guy."

Kelly Hammond, her face a pale mask and her eyes wide and staring, merely nodded.

Angi reached for her portable radio. "Detective 74. 10-68 L20 on TAC 2." She needed to communicate directly with Sergeant

Simmons to get additional officers to the rental house as soon as possible.

"Ted," she said when Simmons had acknowledged and changed his radio frequency selector to the direct communication channel. "I have a lot of blood on the back door of this house. We have enough to break in to see if there's anyone hurt in there."

"I'm on my way and I'll bring three or four officers," the supervisor said. "ETA two minutes."

Minutes later, uniformed officers surrounded the dilapidated house.

"Remember, guys," Sergeant Simmons said, "we are entering on exigent circumstances, looking for anyone injured. You can only look in places where a person might be but anything you see in plain sight can be used by the detectives to get a search warrant."

The officers nodded and a burly officer named Thompson moved forward. "I'll kick the door for you, Detective."

As Thompson leaned back to put the full force of his 250 pounds behind the kick, Angi said, "Just a minute, officer. We don't want to destroy any evidence if we can avoid it." With that, she tried the door knob. The unlocked door opened into the kitchen of the house with a squeal from the rusted hinges.

"Gawd, this place stinks," Thompson said. The kitchen sink was filled with dirty dishes and the smell of decaying food permeated every corner. There was no obvious sign of violence in the room, except that the kitchen floor showed smears of blood which appeared to lead toward a narrow doorway.

"I think that doorway might lead to a basement," Jared said. Basements were unusual in the earthquake prone region around Santa Rosa, but a few old houses like the Victorian had them.

"Everyone, be careful not to step in any of this blood on the floor," Angi said as the uniformed officers entered behind her.

"Fan out and check every room for any sign of a body or body parts. Don't touch anything else and report back what you find. Officer Hagen and I will take the basement."

Hagen took the lead as the two descended the narrow stairway. It was impossible to avoid stepping in the blood on the stairs but Hagen and Masters tread as carefully as they could, mindful of the likelihood of compromising evidence with every step.

Hagen reached the bottom step and splayed his flashlight beam around the room. Angi, two steps behind him said, "Holy shit, Jared! That's far enough. Unless you see a body, we need to back out and get a search warrant."

Hagen shook his head and began to step backward, retracing his path up the stairs as closely as possible, with Angi doing the same just above him. As they reached the top of the stairway, the other officers were carefully filing back through the kitchen and out the back door.

"Anything?" Angi asked when the group reassembled outside. Every officer except Hagen shook his head.

"Well, Jared and I did find something. Sarge, we need a tight perimeter around this house. No one inside except me, another violent crimes detective, or the lab people."

Sergeant Simmons nodded and motioned to three officers, who took up positions around the house. "What did you find?" he asked.

"A slaughter room, Sarge," Hagen answered. "That's the only way I can describe it. It's been used recently — and not for an animal."

Chapter 6

10:16 a.m. — June 29. "That's right, Mike," Angi said when she met with her supervisor outside Hammond's house. "We need to keep this off the air as long as possible. I don't want a crowd gathering around here. The crime scene is just too sprawling to keep everyone out if we had a mob like they had up at the fire scene."

"Well, if there's any good news about the fire, it's receded but still going strong enough to keep most of the hard-core looky-loos up on Fountaingrove for awhile," Garrison said. "Devon is just clearing from the 211 and I've paged him to meet you here. Do you need any other detectives?"

"Yeah, I'd like to have Julie come out to coordinate another sweep of the area. I want to be sure we don't miss anything. I don't know for sure what happened here but it's a massive crime scene."

"OK, I'll see what I can do. I'll page you with Phelps' ETA as soon as I get her rolling."

Angi nodded and then turned her attention to the front porch where Hammond was standing.

"Thanks for letting me come into your house, Ms. Hammond."

"You're welcome, Detective," the neighbor said. "I overheard some of your conversation. Do you think someone was killed in the house next door?"

"Don't worry, ma'am. We're not sure exactly what happened but I'm sure there's no danger now." *That's only a little lie,* Angi thought. *Don't know exactly what happened, but if the blood around the neighborhood and the blood in the basement all belong to one person, he, or she, is definitely dead. No doubt about that.*

"Whatcha got?" Kim asked as she walked up. "Sergeant Simmons sent me down here."

"Excuse us, Ms. Hammond," Angi said as she gently guided Kim away from the woman's earshot.

"More blood than I've ever seen at a scene, Kim. We need to know if it's from more than one person, if you can do that. I'm pretty sure that whoever the blood belongs to, if it's only one or two people, they're dead. Jared and I didn't see any sign of a body but it looks like a butcher shop in the basement of that house. And, of course, anything else you can tell us would be great."

"I'll get right on it. I also sent Aaron to the ME's office with the hand. I was able to pull a good set of prints from it, and Aaron will run those for a match. If it's someone in the system, we should have an ID in an hour or so."

* * *

Dr. Winston Woodward was a legend among California medical examiners. He had retired after a long and celebrated career as the chief medical examiner of San Bernardino County in Southern California. After his retirement, he had moved to Northern California and the relative tranquility of the Sonoma wine country.

Unlike more populous counties, Sonoma County did not experience a level of questionable deaths for which the law required a medical examination. Therefore, the county did not have a full-time medical examiner's office. The Sheriff-Coroner contracted with a private forensic firm for medical examiner services. The workaholic Woodward — 'retirement' was merely an abstract concept to him — was quick to join the firm on a part-time basis. He soon became the 'go-to' medical examiner for the county's highest profile cases.

"I must say, Aaron, you usually bring me more than a hand to work with," the doctor said with a wry grin.

"I know, Doc, but it's all we have now. Anything you can tell me would be great."

"Well, without much examination, I can tell you that it's the hand of a female of slight build. It was violently severed, probably in one blow from a pretty sharp instrument."

"That was one of our questions. Male or female? We have a witness who heard screams last night, He thought that the voice was high and shrill, more like a woman than a man. But he said it could have been a man in panic."

"Well, this is definitely female. The finger structure is thinner and more tapered than I would expect to see on a man's hand, even of this size. The hair on the hand is also finer than would be on a man's. Also, while not conclusive, the manicured nails are more indicative of a female. But I see that the fingers have been inked, so I presume you are already in the process of checking for fingerprints."

"Right on, Doc. Kim rolled a set before we iced the hand to bring it in. I'm going to run those when I leave here. Can you tell me anything about the weapon?"

"I'll have to examine the bony structures more closely to be definitive, but my educated guess is something heavy and very sharp. Good candidates would be a meat cleaver, a machete, or even a Samurai sword."

Chapter 7

11:42 a.m. − June 29. "What did you find, Kim?" Angi asked as the lab tech emerged from the rental house.

"Let's take a walk-through. I think your description of the room as a slaughter house was very apt," Kim said as the women entered the house and walked to the basement. "I have little doubt that someone was killed down here, and it probably happened last night. See there. The blood pools are congealed but not dried yet."

"One victim or ...?"

"I can't tell yet for sure. I took blood samples from a couple dozen sites around the room here but until I can get them typed, I won't know for sure how many people are involved. Even then, it will be a minimum number. It's possible a perp was also cut − likely, I'd say, considering the violence that had to go with that much blood-letting. Of course, there could be perps who weren't cut, but I'll be surprised if any victim walked away."

"It seems like at least one victim was trying to run away from it."

"True, but look over here. See this corner where it looks like someone has been a captive for a while. There's that dirty mattress on the floor. And in the back there − it looks to me like an ankle restraint hooked by a chain to a water pipe."

"Sure does. So whoever was here was chained to the pipe, and there are no windows in this area."

"And there's only one ankle cuff and chain, so I'm thinking there was only one victim. It's also likely that no one would have heard her cries, even if she wasn't gagged, since there are no windows in this part of the basement. Now check this out. There are also some bloody ropes there on the floor near this support column. These marks on the column look like rope marks to me.

"My feeling is that someone was tied to this column at some point, and possibly tortured. There's dried blood on the column, right there and it's much older than the pools we see. And look here. Doesn't it look like there is a void on the column where something — I think a person's body — shielded the column from the blood spatter?"

"Good eye, Kim. I have to agree with you."

"I think that the victim was probably here for a while, and she was probably a captive in the basement. She was probably injured here, enough to be bleeding, but somehow managed to escape. She got out of the house and was running around the neighborhood trying to get help. But the perps — I say multiple because it would seem a lot harder for one perp to control someone trying that hard to alert help — caught up with her.

"And I think slightly injured at first because of the bloody handprint on the Douglas's door. If the hand I found in the bushes belongs to the same victim that was at the Douglas house, then it had to be still attached at that point."

"You keep saying 'her,' Kim. Are you sure the victim is female?"

"Pretty sure, based on the size of the hand. But Doc Woodward will confirm that."

"Well, your theory makes sense," Angi said as the women walked back outside. "So the victim was trying to get Douglas's attention by screaming and banging on the door but the perps were closing in on her. She got away, but was being chased around the neighborhood, leaving the blood droppings that the unis found. Then she gets to the other house and gets cornered in the bushes. She leaves a handprint on the window but then one of the perps has some kind of a sharp weapon and lops her hand off right there."

"That's kind of how I read it. Most likely, the victim passed out from a combination of blood loss and plain shock after the hand was cut off. She was probably carried back to the perp's house and dragged through the kitchen. I should mention that the blood smears on the kitchen floor are directional and support the idea that someone who was bleeding profusely was dragged from the back door toward the basement stairs. She had to still be alive at that point for the blood to still be pumping out of the body, although possibly not from the severed hand."

"Because of the traumatic amputation?"

"Right. But remember that she was probably cut significantly somewhere else on her body, because the hand certainly had to have been attached when she was at the Douglas's door. But she was still leaving blood there."

"And there's no sign of a body down there? You didn't find any body parts?"

"None at all. But, based on the amount of blood, I'd say ..."

Kim's voice was momentarily drowned out by the roar of a twin-engine airplane flying only a few hundred feet over their heads.

"... that the rest of the body didn't leave here in one piece."

* * *

For Lieutenant-Colonel Gus Passmore, it was a dream job. The retired Air Force pilot had flown in some of the world's hotspots. There was Vietnam, where he flew the venerable McDonnell Douglas F-4 Phantom supersonic jet in both fighter/bomber and reconnaissance roles. Later, he flew support missions in the Afghan/Soviet conflict and in the First Gulf of Sidra incident.

In 1983, Col. Passmore retired from the Air Force. Almost immediately, he accepted a position flying the Lockheed P2-V aerial tanker for the California Department of Forestry. His job was to pilot a plane capable of dumping up to 2100 gallons of red fire-retardant slurry on range and forest fires. The slurry helped to establish fire lines for ground forces by coating vegetation with a non-flammable glaze.

Passmore enjoyed flying the P2-V and the feeling of accomplishment he received when an aerial drop was precisely placed. For the former bomber pilot, precise placement of a payload was a requirement of the job and he was one of the best. Passmore was attached to the Santa Clara Unit of CDF, operating out of the San Jose airport. But today, he had been assigned to assist the Sonoma Unit in fighting the potentially devastating Mayacamas fire.

His current mission called for an approach from the south with a drop parallel to, and east of the homes off Fountaingrove Parkway. He was the last of three drop planes, designated 'Smokeys,' to follow a lead plane into the drop zone. The lead plane would drop a smoke trail indicating where the drops were to start and the path they were to take.

"On course, Colonel," the co-pilot said over the plane's intercom. "Looks like Smokey Leader is taking us up the 101 highway, then turning east to line up along the west side of Annadel State Park and then over the eastern point of Lake Ralphine. That will put us right in line for ..."

"Smokey Seven, Fire Boss," the plane's radio crackled to life. "Smokey Seven, Emergency!"

"Smokey Seven, go ahead, Fire Boss," Passmore spoke into his microphone.

"Smokey Seven, we've had a flare-up on a spur road running roughly southwest to northeast off Wallace Road. A ground crew is cutoff and surrounded by fire. You're the last plane in this drop sequence so we need you to divert and make your drop on their position!"

"Smokey Leader copy," the pilot of the lead plane acknowledged over the radio. "Good luck, Seven."

"Can you see their location, Pete?" Passmore asked over the plane's intercom, and then acknowledged the radio call. "Roger, Fire Boss. Smokey Seven is breaking off our run and realigning for the rescue drop."

"Got it, Colonel," the co-pilot said. "Turn left, heading three-two-zero. When we intersect that main east-west highway, I'll call your turn to the right to line us up with the spur road."

Passmore pulled the twin-engine plane into a steep turn to the left and also began a gradual descent. In most slurry drops, the goal was to blanket as wide an area as possible to form a fire break. However, in a rescue drop, where slurry was dropped between the trapped firefighters and the encroaching fire, the drop was made from a lower altitude for a more precise placement.

Placement of the slurry was critical. Firefighters could be injured if hit directly by the downpour and the window between the fire and its intended victims was often narrow.

"OK, Colonel, turn right now to zero-three-zero and drop to 400 feet. You should be pretty well lined up on their position."

"Got it, Pete. I see where they are." Passmore nudged the throttles forward, increasing their speed through the air. The move would hasten their arrival over the stricken firefighters but would probably elicit complaints from people on the ground as the airplane roared low overhead.

It was a complaint the flyer was willing to weather under the circumstances.

Chapter 8

1:43 p.m. – June 29. Ninety minutes later, Angi was back at her desk in the Violent Crimes Unit. The scene had yielded precious little information about what had occurred the night before, but there were some positive aspects.

"Kim got a good print from the handprint on the window," she told Sergeant Garrison. "And of course, she printed the severed hand and got some good prints from that. They're a match. I'm waiting now to see if she comes up with a name, but our victim is almost certainly female."

"What about witnesses?" the sergeant asked. "I saw patrol officers knocking on doors but I didn't hear if they got anything."

"Pretty much a bust on that. Other than Douglas, the guy who called it in, no one else was even aware of anything going on. One guy was upstairs in bed and heard some screams, but thought it was coming from a TV downstairs that his kid was watching. Turns out the kid fell asleep and didn't hear anything either. But otherwise, we got nothing from the neighborhood."

"What about the rental house?"

"Other than the fact that there obviously was a bloodbath in there, we don't have much yet. There was evidence that someone was tied up and tortured. Looked like someone had been tied to a pillar, based on the blood voids on it. But unless and until Kim can sort out the blood evidence or get a hit on the prints she found in the house, we're stalled there too. And that's not looking too good. The few prints she got were not in the blood, and could have just as easily been left by the owners or a former renter.

"My next move is to try to contact the property management company and get a name on whoever rented the house. Being

Saturday, I don't know if they will be open, but I'll try to find someone. Maybe that will give us an ID on our reclusive guy and maybe even his associate or associates."

"OK, go for it. I know with that much blood, there's little likelihood that the victim is still alive, but we can't assume that — not yet."

* * *

Angi picked up her purse and started for the door. She had considered calling the property management company but decided she would just make the short drive to their office. She would need to see the rental records in any case, so she might as well see if they were open on Saturday.

She was only a few feet from her desk when a voice called from the stairway at the back of the office. "Detective Masters, wait up."

Angi turned with a smile. Had the first break in the case had finally come? "What you got, Aaron?"

The lab assistant didn't return the smile. "No luck, Detective. Doc Woodward is certain the victim is female, just as Kim thought, but the prints don't match anything in any database that we can access."

"Damn it! Ok, thanks, Aaron. I was just on my way out to talk to the property managers to see what I can find out about the renter. If I get anything that might point to a female in that house, I'll let you know."

* * *

"Thanks for coming down so quickly," Angi said as Max Detwiler, the owner of Detwiler Property Management approached the front door of his business. Angi had found the business closed when she arrived. It had actually taken longer for the dispatcher to locate a home phone number for the owner than for him to arrive in response to her call.

"No problem, Detective," Detwiler said. "I saw something about what happened on the news. I wondered if it might involve the Kalder house when I heard the location. The renter struck me as pretty strange, but he had all the IDs required by the state and the owners to rent the property."

Detwiler quickly located the property file. "Here it is, Detective. As you can see, I wrote down his California driver's license number, the address on his driver's license, and his Social Security number on the application form. He paid the initial rent plus a one month deposit with cash. It looks like he sent a cashier's check issued by Fifth Sonoma Bank for the rent for next month. I still have it in the file. I just didn't have time this past week to get to the bank with my deposits."

"Could you make me a copy of all of those documents, Mr. Detwiler? I'd really appreciate it."

* * *

As soon as she got back to her car, Angi switched her radio to the information channel. "Detective 74. 10-27 and 29 on Parker, Robert LeRoy. DOB 2-29-54. California DL number Q3141592." She was asking for verification of the driver's license info provided by Detwiler, as well as any wants or warrants on the renter, Parker.

A few moments later, the radio crackled to life. "Detective 74. Regarding your California DL Q3141592. That's an invalid number. Also, there is no record of subject Parker with a DOB of 2-29-54 in any system, including driver's license, motor vehicle registration, and property records. No outstanding wants or warrants in that name."

Just as I suspected, Angi thought. *Phony DL, phony name.*

"10-4," she said. "Could you call Inyo County Sheriff and confirm the address of 9476 Mazourka Canyon Road in Independence?"

Any bets on that being a valid address? she thought as she waited for a response. *Not a bet I would take.*

Ten minutes later, the radio answered her bet. "Detective 74. Inyo reports that address is invalid. They said that if it did exist, it would be nothing more than scrub bushes and sand."

Chapter 9

2:15 p.m. — July 4. Dr. Charley Stivers enjoyed nothing more than a quiet day of fishing. The 55-year-old dentist had taken some extra days off to enjoy his favorite pastime. His mind wandered aimlessly as his 18-foot bass boat drifted in the calm waters of the lower end of Lake Sonoma.

Created three years previously by the damming of Dry Creek, the reservoir quickly became a popular recreation area for boaters and fishermen. Most of the pleasure boaters preferred the wider expanse of water in the northwest part of the lake behind the Warm Springs Dam.

That was fine with Stivers. It meant his favorite fishing spot, a cove and adjacent area on the south end of the high bridge near the dam, was relatively peaceful and the water quiet, even on a holiday.

As the boat drifted near the back of the cove, Stivers' daydreaming was interrupted by a *thunk* as the boat bumped against something in the water.

"Damn lazy people!" Stivers swore as he sat upright. It was not the first time he had encountered plastic bags of trash floating in the water, thrown overboard by careless boaters. This time, though, the floating container was a large green plastic bag, the kind normally used to dispose of grass clippings or other yard waste. But like the others he had found, it was tied tightly and the air trapped inside allowed the bag to float.

"Shit! Some asshole must have had a big party on his boat," Stivers said as he reached to pull the bag aboard his boat. He grabbed the knotted top of the container to flip the dark green trash bag into the bow of his boat.

"What the ...?!" he said aloud. Never had he pulled a bag this heavy from the water.

Bracing himself, Stivers grabbed the plastic sack with both hands and heaved it over the side and into the bow space. As soon as the bag landed, Stivers jumped backward, almost falling overboard. A corner of the plastic had snagged an oarlock and tore. When the bag came to rest, a human foot protruded from the torn corner.

* * *

The five days since Angi arrived at the gruesome scene off Sebastopol Road had produced no new leads and the case was at a dead end. There wasn't even a body to confirm that a homicide had actually occurred. However, the volume of blood at the scene and particularly in the rental house seemed to make that a reasonable conclusion.

Angi had confirmed that the California driver's license used by the man who called himself Robert Parker was, in fact, a forgery. Officials at Fifth Sonoma Bank confirmed that the cashier's check sent to the property manager was also a forgery. Neither of those pieces of information helped much in determining what had happened in the normally quiet neighborhood.

Firefighters had contained the Mayacamas fire on Sunday and by Monday the blaze was listed as extinguished. Fortunately, there was no damage to the homes off the Fountaingrove Parkway, except for two small outbuildings which had burned. Life in Santa Rosa, it seemed, had returned to normal.

Angi sat on a bench next to a hammock swing in her 'Fortress of Solitude,' as she called it. It was one of Angi's crowning additions to her residence, and a nod to George Reeves. As a child in the 1950's, Angi often joined the boys in her neighborhood to watch the weekly TV show, *The Adventures of Superman*, with Reeves in the lead role.

Nestled in a back corner of her yard, the fortress appeared to be a flowered island at the edge of a sea of green. The prominent features were roses of varying sizes and varieties, mostly planted by Angi's mother. Concealed among the rose bushes and other greenery was a meandering path of stepping stones, cross-sections of a California redwood tree.

The path led to the corner of her property where a hammock swing sat next to a four foot high water feature, complete with a flagstone waterfall and a bubbling pond. Even though her house was visible from the swing, the place still gave her refuge and the gentle sounds of the water helped her think.

Sitting on the stone bench, the quiet bubbling of the water in her ears, Angi sipped a glass of her favorite wine, V. Sattui's *Gamay Rouge*. Even though she was off-duty on this holiday, her mind was actively going over every aspect of the strange case.

"Damn!" she swore out loud. "No matter how I look as this thing, I can't see where to go with it next!"

She stood and wandered slowly down the stepping stone path toward the house, sipping the last drops of the strawberry-hinted fluid. Her thoughts were suddenly interrupted by the jangle of her telephone.

"Masters," she said.

"Angi, this is dispatch. We just got a call from Sergeant Dave Masters at the Sheriff's Office. He wants you to meet him right away at the marina on Lake Sonoma. Do you know how to get there?"

"Yeah. Canyon Road out of Geyserville to Dry Creek Road, right?"

Why would her uncle want her to come to the lake? "Do you know what's up?" she asked the dispatcher.

"Apparently some fisherman found a plastic bag floating in the water and there's a dismembered body in it."

Chapter 10

3:55 p.m. — July 4. *I'm glad I didn't finish that wine,* Angi thought, even though adrenaline countered the mild buzz of the alcohol. *This probably isn't going to be pretty and I'd hate to puke up a $21 bottle of wine.*

Angi steered her unmarked detective car up the on-ramp to U.S. 101, its siren wailing and the Federal 'fireball' light on the roof flashing a red warning. Twenty-six minutes later, she guided her car into a knot of sheriff's cars and an ambulance assembled in the marina parking lot.

"You got my victim, Uncle Dave?" she asked as she approached the brown-uniformed supervisor.

"Well, we certainly have somebody's victim. I called you because I don't know of any other possible dismemberments lately, but it will be tough to confirm. A fisherman, the guy over there with the deputies, thought he was being conscientious in pulling a bag of trash from the lake. The bag was still in the boat when my guys arrived."

"Why do you say it's tough to confirm?"

"The fisherman says the bag was tied up tightly, enough that it floated. But when we opened it, the head and both hands are missing. I feel certain that they were never in the bag because it was tied too tight for anything like that to have slipped out.

"The torso was also missing, but one of my guys found it on a rock outcropping just below the south end of the bridge. It's a woman, probably young from the looks of the torso. There's also blood on the bridge railing just above the outcropping.

"Looks to me like the perp dismembered the body," Dave said. "Then he put the parts in the bag, minus the head and hands, and threw it and the torso off the bridge. He probably hoped everything would sink to the bottom of the lake. Fortunately for us, the bag hit the water but floated, and the torso hit the outcropping instead of going into the water."

"You say you're missing both hands. We might have one of them in our evidence cooler. And I suppose there are no tats or other marks on the torso."

"Nothing that we could see, although the skin is kind of shriveled and darkened from lying in the heat. We'll have to get the ME's opinion, but my guess is that the torso has been there for a few days, generally coinciding with your crime scene."

"Is the media onto this yet?"

"Right in the middle of it. There was a reporter from the Santa Rosa Sun at the marina with his family when the fisherman came ashore. Paul Hackworth, if you know him. He's being cooperative, but the story will get out."

"Yeah, I know him. That's probably not a bad thing. We don't have much to ID the victim, this one or mine, or even know for sure yet if they're the same person. It's probably gonna take a call from some worried family member to give us a lead. I'll talk to him, though. Maybe I can get him to sit on the story for a day or so to see if the ME can get some kind of ID from what we have."

* * *

The following morning, Angi was at her desk in the Violent Crimes Unit before 7:30 a.m. She really wasn't sure why she felt the need to be at work that early — she could do nothing until she heard from Dr. Woodward. Still, the walls at home seemed to be closing in, urging her to get to work to solve her latest case.

It was nearly 10:00 a.m. when the medical examiner finally called. "Give me some good news, Doc."

"I don't know if it would be considered good news, Angi," the pathologist said, "but I can tell you some things about the victim from Lake Sonoma. Of course, the victim is female. Judging by the relative development of the body and condition of the skin, I would say she was between 16 and 22, with an edge toward the low end of that.

"The cause of death was most likely a stab wound to the heart. It's a single puncture wound and is unusual because the blade was triangular in shape and very sharp on the edge. I have some ideas, but I need to research it a little more."

"Any idea who she was?"

"The only thing that could be considered an identifying mark is that her lower left arm has been broken in the past. From the way the bone is knitted, I'd say it happened when she was very young. It was probably what we call a 'greenstick' fracture.

"She has also been raped recently. Judging from the tearing and bruising around the vagina, I'd say multiple times over the past eight or ten days. There is also evidence that she has been held captive. There is a serious abrasion on her left ankle, probably left by some kind of metal clamp or cuff around her leg. Of course, I can only speculate that the cuff was attached to some solid object."

"That would fit with what Kim found in our crime scene. There was a metal cuff attached to a chain which was locked around a pipe. The cuff could be locked with a padlock, although we didn't find one. Was there any evidence of torture?"

"Funny you should mention that. Yes, although it was done in a strange way. I found very thin cuts, probably consistent with a razor blade, on the underside of each of her breasts. There was also one small cut on the outer edge of the left areola, probably made with the same instrument. There were no other cuts on the body. Well, other than the dissection, of course. However, there is some evidence that the victim was bound by the neck.

"Of course, her head is missing, but the small amount of her neck that was left after her head was severed shows signs of rope burns. Also, there are some abrasions on the upper arms and upper chest which could be rope marks as well. I'd say she was probably bound around the neck and across the upper chest and then the attacker made the cuts on her breasts. Why he would lift the breasts and cut on the lower part of them is beyond anything I've ever seen before."

"That's also consistent with the evidence at my crime scene. So now the sixty-four dollar question, Doc. Is the body from Lake Sonoma my victim from the Roseland area?"

"One of the reasons it took so long for me to get back to you was the time it took to microscopically compare the lower arm of the dismembered body with hand from your scene. There are some small inconsistencies, quite probably as a result of the arm being banged on something after the hand was severed.

"But there are enough points of matching bone surfaces that I can say with reasonable certainty that the hand Kim found in the bushes came from this arm."

Shit, Doc. 'Yes' would have been sufficient, Angi thought, but she said, "Thanks, Doc. I appreciate all your work."

Angi hung up the phone and sank back in her chair. *A headless body of a tortured girl with no match on fingerprints, killed by an asshole we also can't identify. Where do I go next?*

Chapter 11

11:10 a.m. — July 5. "I just don't see any other way to do it, Mike," Angi told Sergeant Garrison. "Chances are, this girl, or maybe young woman, is reported missing. But with no prints on file anywhere and no way to match her face with any flyers, the only thing I can see to do is have the media run an appeal."

"You're right, Angi, but I just want to make sure you understand the downside. With very little description — hell, we don't even have a hair color — about all we can say is a woman missing in the last two or three weeks who's about five-foot-one, and maybe in her late teens or early 20's. There could be a lot of panicked people out there thinking it's their daughter, wife, or sister."

"I know that, but otherwise, we have at least one family who's missing someone who will never have a resolution unless we try."

"I wish I had another option for you, but I can't think of anything else besides a public appeal either. Are you going to use that reporter from the Santa Rosa Sun?"

"Yeah, I think he deserves to get a bone first. He's been cooperative in withholding the discovery since yesterday."

Garrison nodded and turned back to his office as Angi picked up her phone.

"Paul, this is Detective Angi Masters," she said when the reporter answered his phone. He had given her his direct contact number the day before when she had asked — almost begged — him to sit on the story of the discovery of the dismembered body. "I need to talk to you about yesterday. Do you have time to meet?"

"Of course. How about Fremont Park in 30 minutes?"

The small park was about half way between the police department and the newspaper office. It would afford the detective and the reporter a quiet, and neutral, place to talk.

"Thanks for meeting me, Paul," Angi began when they were seated at a secluded park bench near a soccer goal. "I need your help."

"I was going to call you anyway. I've sat on this thing as long as I can. My editor is after me to go to print with the dismembered body story. That's big news, especially for Santa Rosa. I can't hold it any longer."

"I understand and I'm not asking you to. What I would ask that you do is just to temper it as much as you can. We are pretty sure the victim is a young woman who has probably never been in trouble. She was probably kidnapped in the past two or three weeks and held in this area. But we don't know where she's from."

"What about fingerprints? Can't you identify her that way?"

"We've tried but she's not in the system. Like I said, she's probably never been in trouble before. I'm asking you to be circumspect in your story because it will be devastating news to some family. But even more so, there might be other families who might suffer needlessly thinking their loved one is the victim."

"I understand, and I think I can sell that angle to my editor. But what about a photo or at least a sketch of her face. That would help a whole lot."

"Yes, it would. The thing is — and I'm asking you to handle this part as delicately as possible — her head is missing."

* * *

Three days later, Sergeant Garrison sat on the edge of Angi's desk. "Anything from the news appeal? I thought Hackworth did a pretty good job with the story."

"Shit, no," Angi said. "We've had twenty or so calls over the weekend, but nothing solid. It seems that there are a ton of teens and young adults out there who had greenstick fractures of their lower arms as little kids. So that description is getting us nowhere.

"And I'm no further at figuring out who our mysterious Robert Parker really is. Julie and I went back to the rental house on Saturday morning but we can't find anything that leads us to his true identity."

"OK. I know you're doing your best. Just keep me informed."

Angi nodded and then resumed leafing through the case file on her desk. *What am I missing? There has to be a lead to the killer in here somewhere.*

She was so deep in concentration that she was startled when her phone rang.

"Detective? My name is Gus — August — Passmore. Your dispatcher transferred me to you."

"Yes, Mr. Passmore. This is Detective Angela Masters. How can I help you?"

Passmore briefly described his background and duties, including the emergency drop for the stricken firefighters.

"As I was turning to the northeast to line up on my rescue drop, I flew over an area where there were a whole bunch of police cars. Obviously, we were going too fast to see much, but I was a little concerned that I might disturb something the police were working on, maybe an interview or something, with my low overflight. But, of course, it couldn't be helped under the circumstances. Anyway, I looked down for a second as we flew over."

"Yes, sir?"

"I remember seeing two women standing near some kind of van with *Crime Lab* stenciled on the roof. As we flew past, I thought I spotted something on the roof of a house near where that van was parked. But then I had to get my attention back on the drop."

Angi nodded silently. *I don't want to interrupt at this point, but where is this going?*

"It was just a fleeting glimpse, and I wasn't sure of what I might have seen, so I didn't give it much thought again. But then I saw in the newspaper where the police found a hacked-up body, and that maybe not all the parts were there. So I thought I'd better call in."

"And what did you see, Colonel?"

"I could be mistaken, Detective. I mean it seemed pretty surreal outside a war zone, downright crazy even. But the house immediately to the east of where the crime lab van was parked that day, I'm fairly sure now that there's a human head on the roof of that house!"

Chapter 12

10:17 a.m.   July 8. Angi hung up the call and promptly punched the numbers for Kim's direct line. "Remember when we were standing outside the rental house next to your van and a plane flew very low overhead?"

"Yeah, I do. The noise drowned out something I was telling you."

"And your van was parked between the rental house and the house where the woman let me into her back yard, right?"

"Yeah, I think so. What's going on, Angi?"

"I just got a call from the pilot of that plane. He was making a retardant drop on the fire but when he flew over, he thought he spotted something. He dismissed it then, not thinking it was real. But now ..."

"Tell me!"

"He thinks our victim's head is on Kelly Hammond's roof!"

* * *

Twenty minutes later, Angi and Kim pulled to the curb in front of Kelly Hammond's house. Before they could get out of Angi's car, the fire department engine pulled to the curb behind them.

"Thanks for the quick response, Captain," Angi said, greeting the engine supervisor. "If you will keep your crew here for a couple of minutes, I'll contact the homeowner."

Angi approached the house, but Kelly was already out on her front porch, attracted by the noise of the fire engine's diesel engine idling at the curb.

"Detective Masters. What's going on?"

"Ms. Hammond. We got a tip that there may be some evidence on the roof of your house. I need your permission for the fire department to put up a ladder and climb up there to look."

"You know I'll cooperate, but what makes you think there's something up there?"

"A pilot spotted something that seems worth checking out. We're not sure what we have but we need to look." She turned and nodded to the fire captain, who motioned to two firefighters. They removed an extension ladder from the side of the apparatus and hoisted it into position against the eave of Hammond's house."

"What's up there, Detective?" Hammond asked again, her face a mask of deep concern.

"We're not sure, Kelly. It could be nothing but we just need to check it out."

Angi turned to confer with the firefighters but the hoseman, the junior member of the four-man engine crew, was already stepping onto the roof, while the engineer steadied the ladder. A few minutes passed before the firefighter on the roof appeared at the edge opposite the ladder's location. The nightmare Angi had hoped to avoid came true.

"Hey, Cap," the firefighter yelled. "The cops were right. On the back side of the roof, there's a woman's severed head up here!"

Kelly Hammond fainted onto the front lawn.

* * *

"I'm sorry, Detective," the fire captain said. "I told them to observe and report but I thought they understood that I meant 'report discretely.'"

"Guess not!" Angi hissed through clenched teeth as she moved toward Hammond's prone figure.

Kim was already scrambling up the ladder holding a large brown paper bag, which she would use to collect the head. There was no question it was her responsibility. She was the crime scene technician, but she was also well aware of Angi's acute acrophobia. Best to let the lead investigator tend to the shocked homeowner.

"DellaSerra!" the fire captain barked to the engine driver, "Give the detective a hand with that woman while I call an ambulance."

The wail of the ambulance siren rapidly approached as Hammond began to regain consciousness. Just as the woman's eyes opened, Angi was aware of another woman standing over her. "Kelly! Are you okay? What happened here?" Sonja Douglas's voice growled.

"Mrs. Douglas?" Angi said as she rose to meet the speaker, while the firefighter continued to tend to Hammond. "Kelly will be okay. Someone said something they shouldn't have and she fainted, but she's coming around. An ambulance will be here in a minute to check her out to be certain everything is okay."

"So someone screwed up on this case again?" Sonja Douglas said, the contempt in her voice uncontrolled. "First, you can't even send police to help when my husband called about the person at our door. Then, you tell Kelly that there's no danger when some woman was butchered in the house next door, probably by a guy that she can identify. And now, 'someone said something they shouldn't have,' and my friend is out cold on the ground. You people don't give a shit about the folks who live here!"

Angi looked at DellaSerra, whose eyes showed that he understood. *I've got this, Detective. I'll take care of the woman. Go ahead and deal with the upset neighbor.*

"Let's go over here, Mrs. Douglas," Angi said, motioning the woman away from the still-prone Kelly Hammond. "I'm sorry you feel that way," she said when they were out of earshot of the others. "We ... I as the lead investigator ... really do care about what's happened here. I know this is a neighborhood of good people and the police rarely have issues in this area. I also apologize on behalf of myself and the department for some snags in this case. I completely understand your concerns and I want you to know I won't try to minimize them. All I can say is that we are truly dedicating our full resources to finding out what happened here."

"It's like we're in a slasher movie here, Detective. I have just been terrified about what might happen to us, or to Kelly, if that man came back."

"That's completely understandable, Mrs. Douglas. But I want you to know that we do have patrol cars cruising through your neighborhood on a more frequent basis until we catch whoever did this. And I can tell you that the man from that house took great effort to disguise his identity, so it's very unlikely that he will come back here and risk being seen."

"All right. Thank you, Detective. I'm sorry for going off on you the way I did."

"It's quite alright, Mrs. Douglas. If you ever have any questions or concerns, please call me right away. I'll do my best to answer any questions you have."

As Sonja Douglas moved to check on her friend, Kelly, Angi thought *A good example of the police sometimes being their own worst enemy. We've had some screw-ups in this case but we gain a lot more by just frankly admitting that than taking the old tact of 'we're the police. We don't make mistakes.' Because we do, and we did on this case — my case. I'm going to do everything I can to find this SOB.*

Chapter 13

3:25 p.m. — July 8. "Were you able to get anything that can identify her, Doc?" Kim asked when Dr. Woodward answered the phone.

Three hours earlier, she had delivered the severed head to the medical examiner, with a request that he expedite his examination. The request was pro forma for Winn Woodward. He knew the importance of identifying the victim.

"Yes, Kim. Can you and Angi come to my office?"

"Good news, I hope," Angi said when she and the lab tech arrived at the ME's office a few minutes later.

"I think so, Angi. First of all, I'm pretty sure she's a teenager, so you're probably looking for a runaway. She had light brown hair and brown eyes. She also has had some dental work, most notably a crown on her #15 molar. That's unusual for someone this age. The work was probably done within the past year."

"Is there any way we can get her cleaned up enough to get a photo of the head that we can use on flyers? At least, maybe we can have a sketch artist look at her and make a drawing. I really need to get this girl identified soon."

"That's a little out of my area of expertise, but let me talk to someone. The owner of Rasterson Mortuary is a golf buddy of mine. I'm sure he would be willing to help us."

* * *

The following morning, Angi stopped at the ME's office in response to a call from Dr. Woodward.

"Detective Angela Masters, this is George Rasterson," Woodward said. "George worked late last night but I think you'll like the results." He led the detective to his office. The bespectacled little man with thinning hair and a distinct limp followed behind.

The head of a young woman lay on a gold velvet pillow on a table in Winn Woodward's small office. The hair was perfectly combed and the eyes were gently closed. The face was expertly made up with subtle applications that disguised the death pallor of the skin. A purple silk scarf covered the lower neck, concealing the severed condition of the head.

"Wonderful work, Mr. Rasterson," Angi said, shaking the mortician's hand. "Thank you, so much. I think this will definitely help us find out who she is."

"Ya .. you're welcome, Detective," the mortician said, intimidated by the blonde investigator who stood nearly a head taller than he was.

"I've already taken several photos for you, Angi," Woodward said, breaking the awkward exchange. "I hope these will work for you."

Angi was still in high spirits when she walked into the Violent Crimes office a short time later. "Mike, check this out," she said after going directly to Garrison's office. "The ME and the owner of Rasterson's did some great work in getting our victim presentable for a flyer."

"Let's get something on paper right away," the sergeant said. "I think this has got to pay off for us."

* * *

By early that afternoon, copies of the identification flyer featuring a headshot of the young female victim had been faxed to every law enforcement agency in the greater Bay Area. Police department clerks would follow up with color copies mailed to the police agencies. Now it was a matter of waiting to see if the flyers generated the hoped-for lead. It didn't take long.

Shortly after 3:00 p.m., Sergeant Adam Spain of the Santa Rosa Police Juvenile Crimes Unit walked up to Angi's desk. "I've got something for you, Angi," he said with a grin. He laid the ID flyer on her desk and next to it, a missing person notice from the Coreyton Police Department.

"I just got this in the mail this morning. It's a little strange, in that the notice says this girl went missing nearly three weeks ago, but the notice was dated and postmarked on Saturday. But in any case, the photo of the missing girl looks like your victim to me."

"Sure does, Sarge. Thanks."

Spain nodded to the approaching Garrison as he walked out of the Violent Crimes office. "Did Adam have some good news, Angi?" Garrison asked as he approached the detective's gray steel military surplus desk.

"Sure did, Mike. I think this is probably our girl. The notice says she's Abigail Susan Borders, age 15. She ran away from Coreyton — wherever that is — about three weeks ago. For some reason, the flyer on her just went out. But without Rasterson's work, we probably wouldn't have made the connection any sooner anyway."

"Coreyton is a little town up in the Sierras near the south side of Stampede Reservoir. I'm not sure if it's in Nevada or Sierra County, but it's on a little side road off Highway 89. I've been through there when I went fishing up at Stampede. It's not much. I didn't even know they had a police department."

"Well, aren't you just a fount of knowledge, Mike?" Angi smiled. "Okay if I take a drive up there tomorrow?"

"Of course, but do you want to give the PD a call first?"

"I don't think so. If this is our victim, and it sure looks to me like it probably is, I need to talk to the parents. I want to know why it took so long to report her missing and of course I need to confirm identity. Doc Woodward gave me dental x-rays that he took for comparison with her dentist's records.

"But above all, there's something about all this that just doesn't add up. I want to meet this Chief Gumpler who signed the missing notice. And I want it to be on my terms."

"I know that look. Maybe you should take Devon or Julie with you."

"I'll be okay, Mike. I can take care of myself."

"I wasn't worried about you, Angela."

Chapter 14

11:10 a.m. — July 10. The three and a half hour trip had taken Angi up Interstate 80 nearly to the Nevada border and then north on California State Highway 89. She had nearly missed the faded and peeling sign that indicated the town of Coreyton was to the right on a potted asphalt road, badly in need of repair.

This place reminds me of Dodge City in 'Gunsmoke,' she thought as she entered the town. Most of the buildings hadn't seen paint in decades. The main street was covered with the same in-desperate-need-of-repair asphalt as the road leading to the town.

The two small side streets that Angi could see were merely coated with oil-soaked gravel. On one side of the main street, a broken concrete sidewalk paralleled the roadway. Consistent with her *Dodge City* impression, Angi was not surprised that the sidewalk on the opposite side was actually made of boards.

On the boardwalk side of the street, she spotted a weathered sign that said 'olice Dept.' A closer look revealed that the vinyl stick-on letter 'P' had left a dirt encrusted glue residue when it fled the sign long ago.

She parked her city-issue Chevy Caprice in a spot next to a sign saying 'Police cars Only' and walked into the single room police station. A rotund man wearing the dark blue uniform of a city police officer turned from a desk in the corner of the room to greet her.

It was all Angi could do to keep from laughing out loud. The policeman — easily 350 pounds of him — wore four general's stars on each collar of his uniform, as well as four larger stars on each epaulet of the blue uniform shirt.

The shirt was unbuttoned at the collar, probably because it was two inches too small to close around the massive neck. The other buttons on the shirt front gapped in various ways, causing the light to reflect off the stains on the shirt in myriad patterns.

"Well, ain't you just a tall drink a-water?" the man said. "What can we do you for?" The man belly-laughed at his own twist of the greeting.

"I'm Detective Angela Masters from Santa Rosa," Angi said, holding out her hand. "I'm here about the missing flyer you sent out on an Abigail Borders."

"Detective, huh?" the man said. "I'm Chief Gumpler. Gal detective? I guess they let girls work juvenile stuff down in Santa Rosa." He did not reach out to shake her hand.

"Actually, I'm a homicide detective," Angi said, dropping her hand. "You can call me Angi."

"Homicide, huh. Ooowee, what's this here world coming to? I guess you think Abigail is dead, huh?"

"It's possible, but that's why I'm here. We have a murdered girl in Santa Rosa and she looks pretty much like the picture of Ms. Borders on your flyer. I'd like to talk to her parents, with you along, of course, just to confirm whether our victim is their daughter."

"Well, they run the hardware store across the street and four doors down. You don't need me along to babysit you, do you, missy? Big city girl detective should be able to talk to us mountain yokels on her own, dontcha think?"

"Sure, Chief, that's fine. One question though. The flyer says that Abigail has been missing for more than three weeks, but you just sent the flyer out last weekend. Why the delay?"

The man turned to face the detective and his face morphed into a vivid shade of red. "You questioning how I do my job, missy? Think you can come up here from the big city and second guess me?"

"No, Chief, of course not," Angi said. *What the hell is behind this reaction?*

"Well, for your information, I held up on bothering anybody until I was sure she was really gone. Abigail Borders has been a pain in my ass since she was ten years old. Always getting into things and misbehaving. I just figured she lit out for the big city to make something better of herself. Figured maybe she was hiring herself out or something, if you know what I mean," the chief snickered. "It sure is better for all of us around here."

"Well, thank you, Chief," Angi said. *It would do my heart good to kick your balls up between your shoulder blades, but thank you.*

* * *

The small hardware store stood out in that it had been recently painted. The sign identifying the business as 'Coreyton General Hardware' appeared to be professionally constructed. Angi had barely entered the front door when she was warmly greeted by a man in his late 40's.

"Welcome to Coreyton Hardware," the man said, extending his hand. "I'm Bill Borders, the owner. I don't think we've met."

"Hello, Mr. Borders. I'm Angi Masters. I'm a detective from Santa Rosa. Chief Gumpler directed me over here."

"Ha! *Chief* Gumpler? Orrin Gumpler isn't a police officer. He's just a security guard hired by the town to keep an eye on things. We're kind of out of the way for the sheriff's deputies to come up here often.

"But you said Santa Rosa. Does this have something to do with my daughter?"

"Yes, sir, it does. Is your wife here?"

"What is it, Detective. What's happened to Abby?" The concern in the man's voice was palpable.

"Please, sir. It would be better if I can talk to both you and your wife. I need to confirm some information before I can say anything for sure."

"O .. OK. Please follow me. We have a little place in the back of the store."

"Did you find our daughter?" Jean Borders asked when the three were seated in the small living room behind the hardware store.

"We might have, Mrs. Borders. That's why I'm here — to determine that. I have a photograph I would ask you to look at but I have to tell you that it will be disturbing." Jean's eyes immediately filled with tears and she looked at her husband for comfort.

Bill couldn't speak. The lump welling in his throat choked off any speech and a good part of his air. But he nodded to the detective and stretched out his hand.

The photo showed just the head of a young woman, her hair meticulously combed, slight indications of make-up on her face. Her eyes were closed and there was a scarf around her neck that Borders didn't recognize.

"Yes, that's Abby," he choked, handing the photograph to his wife. "Is she ... ?

"I have to ask one more question just to be sure. Does your daughter have a crown on an upper left molar?"

"Oh, God!" Jean Borders broke into heaving sobs. Borders nodded his head and then slumped in his chair.

"I'm sorry to have to tell you that your daughter is dead," Angi said, as gently as she could.

Mrs. Borders dropped the photograph and ran from the room, a piteous wail exploding from her throat.

Borders sat still, looking after his wife and then at Angi.

"Go take care of your wife, sir. I'll just wait here until you're ready to talk."

Chapter 15

12:05 p.m. — July 10. The man sat by the dingy window, smoking a cheap cigarette as he watched the activity on the docks near San Francisco's Potrero Hill district. The three-story hotel was one of the few remaining blighted properties in an area which was gradually becoming more upper-middle class.

He had given his name as 'Harry Longabaugh' when he checked in, paying cash for a week's rent. The clerk didn't get, or didn't mention, the significance of the name but it didn't matter. Ever since the man had met a prostitute named Henrietta Place a few weeks before, he had taken gleeful pleasure in using aliases associated with the Butch Cassidy gang.

"Want some coffee?" Etta asked from across the dimly lit room.

"Nah, thanks. I'm just getting bored here. I need to find another girl."

"You've got me," Etta teased.

"You know what I mean. We both would like ..." The man's voice trailed off. *How many young girls have there been since I met Etta? At least three, maybe it was four? I'm not sure.*

They had all been teen-aged runaways, wandering the streets, unable to support themselves but not wanting to admit defeat in their quest for freedom by calling their parents. Etta approached the girls, usually at some type of music event, claiming to be a talent agent with recording contracts to fulfill. Only when the girls had agreed to accompany the woman did they learn the darkest side of being on the street.

I've still got four fake driver's licenses and social security cards. Those damn things cost me a bundle, but were worth it. So that's at least four houses I can rent for ...

"Well, I think we should go further south. Los Angeles, maybe. That last deal was way too close," Etta said. Her playful manner was gone.

The man didn't reply. *Shit, yeah, it was close.* Etta had bungled cutting the girl loose so they could rape and torture her again, and she had bolted out the door. They were just lucky that no one came outside to investigate her screams, especially at that house where she was pounding on the door. Even the nosy bitch who lived next door to the house he had rented for their latest round of perversion hadn't come out.

I got her, though. Just wait until she starts wondering what the stink is. He chuckled out loud. *Etta was really pissed about it, but I got a good laugh from tossing the girl's head onto that bitch's roof after we cut her up.*

The man flopped back on the bed. "OK. South it is. Let's find us another mark."

* * *

This was absolutely the worst part of the job for Angi, or any other cop. Death notifications were usually handled by the coroner, but nearly every homicide detective has had to make the dreaded notification at least once. The sobs of the man and woman in the next room continued unabated for nearly 20 minutes, but it seemed like hours to Angi. There was nothing she could do but sit there in the family's small living room and wait.

Finally, the couple reached the point where they could physically no longer cry, at least at that moment. "I'm sorry, Detective," Bill Borders said as he and his wife emerged, red-eyed, from the adjoining room.

"Please, sir. There is no need to apologize to me. I want you to know that you have my complete sympathy and that I will do everything I can to find out who did this to your daughter."

"What do you need to know, Detective?" The Borders couple sat on a couch across from Angi. She could see that they were anxious to help, despite their grief.

"Let's start by you telling me a little bit about your daughter."

"That's easy," Borders began. "She was a great girl. But I have to confess that I made life tough for her."

"Bill, this is not your fault," Mrs. Borders said.

"I know, but still ... It's like this, Detective. We are originally from the Santa Cruz area. I was an executive with a small electronics company there. But I always enjoyed the mountains — I was raised in Montana — and often came up to this area just to get away from the bay. Then about five years ago, I was up here with a couple of buddies and saw that this store was for sale. It's always done a good business supplying the campers and fishermen who come up to Stampede. They tend to be people who like that the reservoir is off the beaten path.

"Anyway, I talked to Jean and Abby and we decided to buy the place and move up here, at least for the summers. In the winter, we go back to Santa Cruz. But it's pretty isolated up here and as she got older, Abby began to miss her school friends during the summer. This year was the worst. She lobbied us to let her stay in Santa Cruz for the summer but we wouldn't allow it."

"Chief ... er .. Mr. Gumpler made a comment that she had been a problem."

"I suppose from his view that might be true. As you could see, Orrin isn't the greatest physical specimen. Don't get me wrong. He actually does a good job of looking after the businesses here in town as well as the eight or ten cabins that people have out on the shore.

"But he's a wannabe cop. I've heard he has been turned down for several police jobs because of his weight. He complained to me once about Abby mouthing off to him, but otherwise, I think he was just mad that she spent a lot of time just wandering around. He thinks that kids, even teenagers, should be home with their parents all the time."

"Plus he just doesn't like women, of any age," Jean Borders said.

"So what caused her to run away?" Angi asked.

"About three weeks ago, she begged Jean to take her back to Santa Cruz. We told her no, but that she and her mother would be going back the second week of August so she could go back to school. I planned to stay here through September and then close up the store for the winter."

"So we had quite a fight," Jean Borders continued the story. "I told her to go walk it off — she's, was, a little too old to send to her room. But then, it got dark and she never came back."

"We called Orrin and told him about it and he said he would look for her. He called me later that night and said that one of the cabin owners had driven her down to Truckee. That wasn't that unusual, because there are a couple of teen-aged girls down there that she hung out with sometimes. It's only 15 miles or so away. But when we called those girls' parents, they told us that neither girl had seen Abby that day."

"Did you report her missing to the sheriff then?"

"Yes. Well, not directly. See, Orrin kind of acts as a liaison with the sheriff so we told him we wanted to report her as a runaway. He said he would take care of notifying the sheriff.

"We didn't hear anything for the longest time so I asked Orrin last week to check with the sheriff to see if they had heard anything. He told me that there was no information on where Abby was. All we could do was wait.

"We did call the parents of her friends in Santa Cruz and they all promised to call us if she showed up there anywhere, but we haven't heard from any of them either."

"And when did you talk to Orrin?"

"Thursday ... no Friday morning of last week, why?"

"I'm just trying to get the whole picture. I think I have everything I need for now. Here's the number of the mortuary in Santa Rosa where Abby is. The owner's name is George Rasterson. He will do anything he can to help you make arrangements. Again, I'm very sorry for your loss."

Chapter 16

1:08 p.m. — July 10. Angi left the grieving couple and went directly back to the 'olice Dept.' She had one more thing to do in Coreyton.

"What do you want now, missy?" Gumpler said, spit-soaked BB's of his hamburger spewing from his mouth as he talked.

"Mr. and Mrs. Borders reported their daughter missing to you three weeks ago. When did you relay that information to the sheriff, and don't bullshit me. I can check."

"You bitch! I already told you that you ain't got no business questioning how we do things around here." Gumpler pushed his wheeled chair back and began to rise. But before he could get to his feet, Angi took three quick steps toward him. As she moved, her left hand plunged into the open purse slung over her shoulder. The purse strap dropped away and her hand emerged.

With a flashing twist, the balisong in her left hand flew open as she stiff-armed Gumpler's chest with her right. The rotund man plopped back into his chair. Angi's knee was planted firmly against his crotch and the slender knife blade rested half an inch inside his right nostril.

"Sit still! Now, I asked you when you reported Abby missing to the sheriff. And don't wiggle too much. It's a short trip up your nose to your brain, such as it is."

"OK. OK! I didn't report it."

"Never?!"

"No. At first, I figured she probably was holed up with some friend in Truckee and would be back in a day or two. Then I

65

forgot about it until Bill approached me last week. I knew I'd fucked up, so I just made up a poster myself and sent it out."

"Well, here's what you're going to do. First, you're going to tell Mr. and Mrs. Borders the truth about what happened. Then, if you still have a job here, you're going to get rid of that blue uniform because that is reserved for city police officers — *real* police officers," she said with snarling scorn.

"It sounds like people think you're a pretty good *door-shaker*, so you just might keep your job, but that's up to them. It's the only reason I don't arrest your sorry ass right now for impersonating a police officer.

"If you do keep your job, you will only wear a state-approved security guard uniform and not represent yourself as a police officer. Because if you do, I'll come back up here and arrest you myself."

"OK. OK."

With an impressive one-handed flip, Angi closed the butterfly knife and retrieved her purse from the floor.

As she turned toward the door, Gumpler regained some of his bravado. "Yeah, and what if I tell the sheriff that you threatened me with a knife? What then, miss high-and-mighty city *detective*?"

"Threatened you? With a knife? Don't know what you're talking about." Angi smiled demurely. "And who do you think they're going to believe? A decorated homicide detective, or a fat-assed, piece of shit rent-a-cop who didn't make a report that might have gotten a girl found sooner, and maybe saved her life? Think about it, asshole!"

* * *

At the same moment, Kim Williams was receiving far better news. Earlier that morning, she began processing the green plastic garbage bag that had held the dismembered remains found in the lake. While the water had almost certainly destroyed any evidence on the outside of the bag, the tight seal had kept evidence-eating water out of the inside.

Of course, bodily fluids would have compromised evidence on the inside as well, but at least there was a chance that a hair, a fiber, or maybe even a fingerprint might have survived. It was Kim's mission to find out for sure.

It had taken Kim only twenty minutes to find what she was looking for, a fingerprint. It was on the inside of the bag, right where she deduced it most likely would be, in the folds of the top of the bag where it had been tied shut. The knot had protected the print from fluids both inside and outside the bag.

The wait for a match was excruciatingly long, although it actually took a mere two hours for a hit to come back. Kim punched some additional keys on her computer and then gathered up several sheets of paper from her printer.

"Sarge, got a minute?" she said a few minutes later as she knocked on the doorframe of Sergeant Garrison's office.

"Sure, Kim. Come on in. What's up?"

"I know Angi is out of the office today, so I thought you'd better see this. I was able to pull a print from the inside of the plastic bag from the lake and ..."

"Great work, Kim!" the sergeant said as he stood and walked around his desk to sit next to the lab technician. "And I assume you got a hit," he said, eyeing the sheaf of paper in her hand.

"Yes. And Angi isn't going to like it. The print belongs to one Edward Lloyd Teach. He's 35 years old and a former sailor. But he was kicked out of the Navy early in his career for assaulting a civilian. He's been in some minor beefs, but didn't hit the radar until earlier this year. According to the California Bureau of Investigation, he's a suspect in abductions of teen-aged girls in

Merced and San Luis Obispo. He's in the wind now. No one has seen him since he left San Luis Obispo in a hurry last March."

"Do we have a picture?"

"I have a mug shot from an arrest for larceny in Fresno two years ago. He pled to that and served 120 days in the county jail. That's his last official police contact as far as I can tell."

"OK, Devon and Julie are both out on other cases right now. Can you take that mug shot over to Mrs. Douglas and ... what was her name? ... Ms. Hammond? See if they can ID him as the renter."

Kim was not a police officer and this was the first time anyone had asked her to do anything directly related to a case other than lab work. But she was up for the task.

"You got it, Sarge. I'll let you know."

Chapter 17

8:00 a.m. — July 11. Sergeant Garrison called the informal meeting to order in the small room that served as the Violent Crimes unit conference room. "We're here to discuss the case of the homicide on June 29 and the subsequent finding of the body last week up at Lake Sonoma," he said.

"I'll lead off," Angi said. "Thanks to some great work by Kim, Doc Woodward and Mr. Rasterson, we were able to put together a usable photo of the victim. Sergeant Spain was able to tentatively ID her as a runaway from up near Truckee and I confirmed that with her family yesterday. Meanwhile, Kim was able to ID the suspect." She nodded to the lab tech.

"Yes," Kim said. "Each of you has a packet on the perp, an Edward Lloyd Teach. Yesterday, I took an old mug shot of him out to the scene. Both of the women in the neighborhood who have seen him positively identified Teach as the guy who lived in the rental house where the murder took place. They say he's got more of a beard now than he had in that mug shot. He's also a suspect in two other abductions of teen-aged girls but he's in the wind right now."

"Did you have any trouble with either that Douglas woman or the other one — what's her name? Hammond?" asked a man as he entered the room.

"No, Lieutenant. They were very cooperative."

Lieutenant Robert Clews was the investigations commander for the Santa Rosa Police Department. Sergeants Garrison of Violent Crimes, Krohn of Property Crimes, and Spain of Juvenile Crimes reported to him. Only narcotics investigations and internal affairs were outside his realm.

And Lieutenant Clews — 'Clouseau' to many, behind his back, was almost universally derided as an incompetent investigative commander. He rarely left his office, which made this visit unusual in itself.

"Why do you ask that, sir?" Garrison asked.

Clews hated Garrison, whom he considered to be one of the 'golden trio.' Clews had applied to be the chief of police when the job was last vacant, but the promotion went to Jim Hathaway. He hated Hathaway because he was, in Clews' opinion, too 'buddy-buddy' with the troops. And Hathaway had trained Garrison. And Garrison had trained Masters, the third prong of the 'golden trio.'

The way to get your officers to respond was to keep them under your thumb at all times, not being all nicey-nice like the 'golden trio' preach. This department is going to hell with all its 'community policing' bullshit. The city, in Clews' mind, had blown an opportunity to choose him to set things right.

The lieutenant raised his nose as though the answer was obvious. "Well, a couple of screw-ups by the lead investigator at the scene have ignited quite a fire storm of its own in the neighborhood," he said, eyeing Angi as he spoke. "Mrs. Douglas, especially, seems to be leading a movement to make formal complaints to the mayor, city council, media, and whoever else will listen. They are saying that the police don't care about them or problems in their area. And this administration didn't get on top of it from the get-go.

"Of course, if we had handled it right, we could have assured them that he have a good neighborhood. We have stats to show that, first of all, it's not an area that demands a lot of police presence. And we have stats showing that our response time to calls for service in that area is pretty good."

"Except for the night a teen-aged girl was running around screaming for help and leaving bloody handprints on houses," Devon deadpanned. "Is that in your stats, too, sir?"

Clews glared at Anderson and, without another word, slammed his cheap vinyl notebook closed and stormed out of the room.

Garrison shot a disapproving glance at Anderson as the detectives in the room snickered, but the point was made. "Damn it, Devon. Show the man a little respect."

"I'll show the detective lieutenant all the respect in the world, Mike, just as soon as you get promoted into the job. Until then, for you, I will show Lieutenant Clouseau a little respect." *As little as I can get away with,* he thought.

Garrison rolled his eyes and turned to Masters. "Nobody thinks this complaint is going anywhere, but a successful resolution to this case is the best way to calm the feelings of those residents. So what's next, Angi?"

"First off, you can let the El-Tee know that I think I've gotten Mrs. Douglas calmed down since Captain Porter last spoke to her. But if she's still upset, I can talk to her again. I think I have some rapport with her and with Kelly Hammond.

"As for the case, we need more intel about how this guy works. As soon as we're done here, my plan is to call the lead detectives in Merced and San Luis Obispo and set up a meeting with them. My thought is for Devon and I to meet them somewhere convenient for all of us, maybe somewhere around Salinas, later this week to compare case notes.

"I'm thinking of Salinas because it's close to Santa Cruz and we can drop over there and check with some of the victim's friends. I'd like to know if she went there after running away, where else she might have gone, and how and why she wound up in Santa Rosa. That might also give us an idea of where Teach is."

Chapter 18

10:15 a.m. — July 11. Angi had just finished making contact with the lead investigators in the two cities where Teach was also wanted for abducting young girls. In Merced, the 14-year-old victim had been found dead near the Big Rascal Creek. Although the girl had been raped, and evidence pointed to her being held captive for a period of time, the body was not dismembered in any way. The 15-year-old victim that Teach was suspected of abducting in San Luis Obispo was still missing.

As Angi checked her files and made necessary copies for her meeting with the other investigators, an unkempt man shuffled through the public door of the Santa Rosa Police station and made his way to the counter. Even in the hot weather, he wore a dirty, threadbare gray Chesterfield overcoat, tossed away after its affluent previous owner no longer felt it fit his status.

The man's graying beard grew haphazardly from his face and merged with the thin, greasy mop of uncombed hair on his head. Beneath the overcoat, he wore green cargo pants and worn army paratrooper boots.

"May I help you, sir?" the clerk at the counter asked, smiling.

The dirty man spoke in muted, mumbling tones, but the clerk understood what he said.

"One moment, sir," she said. She tried to maintain a pleasant demeanor, but her face reflected her horror as she picked up a telephone. "Detective Masters, this is Sylvia at the front counter. There's a man here who says he's the one who dismembered the girl they found up at Lake Sonoma."

Moments later, Angi entered the reception area from a door opposite the counter. Devon Anderson was not far behind. The man was still facing the clerk and not moving. There was no one else in the reception area.

"Sir," she called out. "I'm Detective Masters. Can I help you?" *I need to get him away from the clerks at the counter, just in case*, she thought.

Without a word, the man slowly turned to his left. His beard-edged lips parted into a sneer, revealing rotted and missing teeth. As he continued to turn, his right hand pulled a short machete from a leg pocket in his cargo pants.

Angi drew her firearm, and commanded, "Put down the knife, sir. We can talk."

The man's sneer morphed into a broad grin. He raised the machete above his head, and with a guttural shriek, he charged across the small room at the detective.

"Oh, shit! Not again!" Angi spat as her mind flashed back eleven years to a downtown alley.

Patrol Officer Angi Masters was walking with another officer, checking the alley for drunks or drug users. They were also alert for others who might be violating the law or who might be in distress in the dark corners that most people never saw.

Near the middle of the block, they came upon the prone figure of a man next to a blue dumpster. As her fellow officer knelt to check on the man's condition, Angi scanned the shadows for any signs of other people.

Suddenly, from out of the shadows under a steel fire escape ladder, a man later determined to be high on PCP emerged with a bellowing scream. He was a mere 20 feet away and Angi barely had a chance to turn toward the sound. Her stomach knotted as she saw that the man had a machete held high over his head as he charged toward her.

Eighteen feet away now. The training gained from hours spent on the pistol range and in mock situations kicked in. Angi's gun was in her hand without her consciously thinking about drawing it from its holster. The other officer turned and reached for his own weapon but his kneeling position and the prone man beside him hampered his movement.

Fifteen feet away. The attacker let out a guttural growl. Angi took up a two-handed shooting stance, the weapon pointed directly at the charging man's chest.

Fourteen feet. Sergeant Linderer, the gruff but caring rangemaster, was standing behind Angi, his spectral voice chiming in her ear as the real man's voice had done so many times on the range. *Squeeze that trigger, Masters. Don't jerk it. Squeeze it.*

Eleven feet. The revolver barked three times in smooth succession. Angi more felt than saw a tight group of .38 caliber shots plow into the attacker's heart. He was dead when he hit the pavement, the machete clattering away ...

Angi's mind was jerked back to the present at the sound of a machete striking not the pavement of an alley, but the adobe tiled floor of the reception area. She had reacted instinctively, with no clear recollection of what had just happened in the lobby. Slowly, her mind refocused on the present as Sergeant Garrison moved up behind her and carefully removed the Smith and Wesson pistol from her hand.

The unkempt man lay dead at her feet, three bullet holes in his chest and one in his throat.

Chapter 19

10:44 a.m. − July 11. "As you know, Angi, procedures have changed since you were last involved in a shooting," Garrison said after he had escorted Angi to the conference room. "Now, it's mandatory that I place you on administrative leave pending the Internal Affairs review. I also have to take your firearm."

"I understand, Mike. I helped write that policy, remember?"

"OK. Captain Kanyid will be down shortly. You know the policy allows you to have another officer in the IA interview with you if you'd like. Do you have anyone you want me to call in?"

"Well, if it can't be you ..." Garrison shook his head. He was her supervisor and thus could not be her support officer in the interview.

"... then I'll take Julie."

Garrison nodded again and started to leave the conference room.

"Mike, can I ask you a question?"

"Sure, as long as it's not related to this incident."

"Well, it is, but not my part."

"OK. I'll answer if I can."

"Devon was out there too. After I got the call from the front desk, I yelled at him to come with me, and I know he followed me into the lobby. He was off to my right side, I think, when the shooting went down. But he never fired."

Garrison nodded. Devon had drawn his weapon but had not fired at the charging man.

"I know something happened several years ago and that Devon got shot," Angi said, "but I've never heard the full story. I just know that he seems really skittish around guns now. I need to know if I can count on him in a situation like this."

"I don't have time to tell you the full story right now, but I think you know you can count on Devon. Maybe he didn't have a good angle today. I don't know.

But in answer to your question, he was shot in the stomach and almost died. The department didn't have procedures for dealing with the stress of being involved in a shooting in those days, so he had to pretty much deal with it on his own. Christina helped a lot, but he didn't have any official support from the department. That's all changed now, of course, but that's the way it was everywhere back then."

"I would expect that Christina would be right in there. As an ER nurse, she's seen her share of violence, at least the outcome of it."

"I'd be lying if I told you that qualification shooting on the range isn't still hard for Devon. Before he was shot, he was the best shooter on the department. You could cover up his shot grouping with a quarter. He's a little off his game now, but he still meets the qualification score. I'm guessing he just had confidence that you would have the situation today handled." Garrison forced a smile. At least he hoped that was the case.

* * *

"Anderson, Phelps. My office," Garrison said as he left the conference room. Both detectives moved into his office, Julie closing the door when they were all inside.

"OK, guys. We have to re-group a little bit for now. Angi will be out of the loop for at the least the mandatory three days of administrative leave, but this case won't wait. Devon, do you have enough info to handle the meeting with the other agencies?"

"Yeah, Mike, I'm fine with it. I don't think Angi had a chance to get everything set up, but I'll make some calls. Kim should have names for the lead detectives."

"Good. Julie, are you at a point in your other cases where you can put a priority on finding out about the guy in the lobby?"

"I'll make time, Boss. If he is the killer, then Angi's case takes a whole new turn. The guy in the lobby is not the guy whose prints Kim found on the plastic bag. I know that much already."

"OK, get on it. Also, Angi wants you to be her support officer for her interview with IA. Captain Kanyid is on his way down to the conference room so I think it will occur in the next half hour or so."

"Happy to do it, Mike."

"Just remember, you're there for support only. You're not a lawyer so just let her tell her story."

"Not a problem. I can't see anything wrong with the shooting, so I don't think there's anything to be concerned about."

Garrison nodded. He felt it was a 'good shooting', too — a straight-forward case of self-defense with no extenuating circumstances. However, officers sometimes got tripped up in small policy violations even though the overall incident was legal and within policy.

And it was well established that officers being confronted by an investigator immediately in the wake of a shooting incident sometimes were in error on some things they reported. This was a direct result of the stress of the situation clouding their memory. It helped to determine the true facts if the officer had another party, who had not been a part of the incident, to support them through the required debriefing.

"OK. Devon, Angi also planned to take a side trip to Santa Cruz, where the victim's family lived during the winter. Maybe she contacted some of her friends there and someone has some idea as to how she might have come into contact with this Teach character."

"On it, Boss."

"Great. Thanks, guys. Oh, and Devon, don't forget that you'll also have to have a debriefing on the lobby shooting with Captain Kanyid, too. You didn't shoot, but you were there."

Devon nodded. He wasn't looking forward to that, even though he too felt that it was a 'good shooting.'

Chapter 20

3:40 p.m. — July 11. Angi sat alone in the conference room. Although she truly felt she had done what she had to do, there was still a sense of trepidation.

Jackson Kanyid was known as one of the fairest commanders who had ever run the IA office. And a year earlier, when a suspect in a homicide had made an unfounded complaint against Angi, Kanyid had seen through the bullshit and backed her to her supervisors and the chief.

Still, this was a first for Angi. When she had killed the man in the alley, there was no procedure in place for a formal internal review like there was now. Her actions had been reviewed by the then-head of violent crimes and the district attorney and had been deemed justifiable. This interview added a new dimension of review, focused on policy rather than solely on whether her actions were justifiable under the criminal law.

"Hello, Detective," Kanyid said when he entered the conference room. "Are you up to talking to me now?"

"Sure, Captain."

"OK. I know this is somewhat new, and I need to advise you of a few things. First of all, just as with my interview regarding the complaint against you last year, you have the right to have a union representative with you during this interview. Do you want someone here?"

"Yes, sir. I've asked Detective Julie Phelps to sit in. She's not an official union representative, but she's the one I'd like to have here."

"That's fine. I saw her out in the work bay when I came in. Let me step out and get her. Since she's not a regular union rep, I have to advise her of her role in this interview as well."

A few minutes later, Kanyid returned accompanied by Phelps. She smiled at Angi and took a seat next to her across the table from the IA commander.

"OK, we'll begin. This conversation will be recorded unless you object," Kanyid said as he laid a portable tape recorder on the table.

Both Angi and Julie shook their heads.

"I need you to respond verbally," Kanyid reminded the women.

"Recording is okay with me," Angi said.

"Me too," said Julie.

"OK, Detective Masters. I need to start by advising you that under the *Garrity* rule, you are required to answer all my questions completely and truthfully. There is no such thing as a fifth amendment protection in this interview. However, you also need to understand that nothing you tell me, nor anything derived from it, can be used in any criminal investigation of this incident."

"I understand, Captain."

"OK. Why don't you start by telling me what happened immediately before you went to the lobby?"

Angi explained how she was working at her desk when she got a phone call from the front counter. "It was of particular interest to me since the man was claiming to have been the killer in the case I'm working on. I was concerned that there might be other citizens in the lobby, so I asked Detective Devon Anderson to come with me."

"And did he?"

"Yes, he followed me into the lobby. We entered by the employee only door, so the subject standing at the counter had his back to us. I saw that there was no one else in the reception area, so my only safety concern was to get him away from the clerks at the front counter."

"And you did that by yelling at him?"

"Yes. I drew his attention to me, although he never spoke or otherwise acknowledged me or Devon."

"And then?"

"As he was turning, he pulled a machete — one of those short ones like they sometimes use in the vineyards — and charged toward me. I drew my weapon and ordered him to stop, but he kept coming. He seemed to me to just be focused on charging me. He didn't say anything other than just yelling something I didn't understand."

"Did you order him to stop?"

"I remember telling him to put the knife down."

"But he didn't do that?"

"No. It was still in his hand until it bounced off the floor when he went down." *At least the captain is experienced enough not to ask something stupid like 'why didn't you just shoot the knife out of his hand?'* Angi thought.

"And why did you shoot, Detective?"

"I think it's pretty obvious that I was in fear for my life, sir. The guy was charging me with a lethal weapon and showed no signs of stopping his attack." *Both times, but I'm not about to admit I was thinking about the alley shooting.*

"OK, Detective. I think that's all I have. Here's the number for the psychologist retained by the department. You'll need to see her to get cleared for a return to duty. That session is completely confidential and for your own welfare, but policy does require that you see her."

Angi nodded, picked up the business card, and left the room without saying a word. Julie quietly followed her out.

"I think that went pretty well, Angi," Julie said when they were alone. "It was a clean shooting."

"I know it was. Thanks for your support, Jules." *I can't admit to anyone, even Julie, that my head wasn't fully on the situation. But I know in my heart that I did what I had to do.* "But the question is still there. Who was this guy and how was he involved in the murder? None of the witnesses has mentioned anyone who looks even remotely like him as being involved."

"That's my assignment. Mike sent Devon to handle your meeting with the other agencies in Salinas and to follow-up in Santa Cruz. My number one job is to find out about the guy in the lobby."

"Good." Angi said. "Let me tell you ..."

"No! You take your mandatory days off, see the shrink, get cleared to come back to duty, and just wind down for a couple days. I know what I'm doing."

"I know you do. I just ... well ..." Angi smiled. *Yeah, Julie does know what she's doing. She's a good detective and for once, I need to step back.* "... Never mind. I'm headed home. See you in a couple days. And thanks again, Jules."

* * *

The next morning, Kanyid was waiting in the chief's reception area at 8:45 a.m.

"Come on in, Jack," Chief Hathaway said. "I assume this is about Masters' shooting?"

"Yes, sir," Captain Kanyid said.

Melissa, the chief's assistant, sat a cup of coffee and the day's edition of the *Santa Rosa Sun* on the chief's desk and quietly closed the door as she left.

"OK, Jack. How's it look?"

"Well, I interviewed Masters yesterday afternoon. I'm sure there's something she's not telling me, but the situation she described meets all the criteria for an in-policy shooting. Later yesterday, I also interviewed the two clerks who were at the counter when the guy came in, and Detective Anderson. The stories are consistent with only the deviations in perception that I would expect to see. Bottom line, it's in-policy."

"And the criminal inquiry?"

"I got a message this morning from Lieutenant Overton at the Sheriff's Office. He led the outside inquiry into the criminal side of the shooting, as our new protocol requires. He also interviewed Anderson and the clerks and presented his findings to the District Attorney. Krupp agrees that the shooting was justifiable. He's not even presenting it to the grand jury."

"Good. And I know this is probably a stupid question, but is Masters actually staying away from the department for her administrative days off?" The chief cracked a knowing grin at the IA commander.

"Surprisingly, it seems that she is. Dr. Arthur left a message for me this morning that she is meeting with Masters this afternoon."

"So you're comfortable with it?"

"Yeah, Jim, I am. Angi's holding something back. Maybe it's her other shooting. There are a lot of similarities between that one and this. Maybe it's her dad. Maybe it's just the case she's working on, especially since the guy in the lobby claimed to be involved. But whatever is in her head, I think she acted appropriately. That's the bottom line."

Hathaway picked up the newspaper. "Is there anything in the *Sun* about it?"

"Just a brief blurb in the local section. Paul Hackworth wrote the story and it's pretty matter-of-fact."

"OK. Get me your report as soon as you can. I'll sign off on it and her return to duty authorization as soon as she does her three days." The chief would admit only to himself that he was glad to have Angela Masters, more than any other detective, on the job.

Chapter 21

11:30 a.m. — July 12. "Got something for me, Julie?" Garrison asked.

"Yeah, Mike. I've ID'd the guy from the lobby."

"Well, that was fast. Is he part of the case?"

"Afraid not. It wasn't too hard to track him down, since he was fingerprinted when he went into the Army. His name was William Allen and he was 40 years old."

"Forty? The guy looked sixty, at least."

"Yeah, but he was only 40. He was in the Army in Vietnam. In 1968, a load of Agent Orange was inadvertently dropped on his platoon's position. According to his son, who I located in San Francisco — he's a junior at USF — Allen was suffering from at least three types of cancer. But his case was one of those denied by the veteran's administration because Allen could not show a direct link to the Agent Orange exposure.

"According to the son, he was getting progressively worse, showing pre-mature signs of aging, and was developing Alzheimer's. His teeth were falling out and he was losing his ability to care for himself at all. A week ago, he walked away from a care facility in Daly City. The son hadn't heard anything about his whereabouts until I called him last night."

"So he's not connected to Angi's case at all?"

"Not at all. Before he left the care facility, he told a fellow patient that he was tired of being a burden to his family. As far as I can figure out, he somehow made his way to Santa Rosa and probably read about the dismemberment in the newspaper. It's shaking out to be a classic case of suicide by cop. He was despondent over his life circumstances but his son said he would never take his own life. So he presented us with a scenario where we were forced to kill him. The son agrees that it is possible Allen would do that in his mental state.

"One thing is absolutely certain, though. He had no part in Angi's case. On the day the fisherman located the body parts in the lake, and for at least six months before that, Allen was in the care facility in Daly City. He is accounted for every day in their records. There is no way he was involved in the crime."

"OK. Thanks, Julie. I'll let Angi know."

God, I hope Angi can handle this. It was a 'good shooting' according to policy and the criminal law, and the guy forced her into the situation. Still, she took the life of an honorably discharged veteran who never did anything other than serve his country.

* * *

Shortly before noon, Devon Anderson parked in the 'police only' area of the Salinas Police Department.

"Thanks for letting us use your conference room, El Tee," he said to the Salinas detective lieutenant.

"No problem, Detective. The guys from Merced and San Luis Obispo are already in there. There's coffee there, and water and juice in the fridge. Help yourself and let one of us know if you need anything else."

"Detective Lance Smith from Merced," the first detective introduced himself when Devon entered the room.

"Mark Morgan, SLO PD," said the second detective, extending his hand.

"Morning, guys. Thanks for coming. I'm Devon Anderson from Santa Rosa. The lead on this case, Angela Masters, couldn't make it, but we really wanted to get a jump on this if we can."

"Yeah. Sounds like we might have a serial," Smith said.

"OK. Let me start off," Devon said. He described the scene in Santa Rosa, as well as finding the dismembered body in Lake Sonoma, and identifying the victim as a runaway."

"Well, there's one thing we didn't know, and that was where it happened," the Merced detective said. "We found a print belonging to this guy Teach on our victim's shoe. It was obvious she was dumped along the creek, but otherwise we didn't have a murder scene. If this guy was renting houses to hold the victims, we should be able to track that down."

"Same in San Luis Obispo. We don't even have a body, but we have Teach on a security video with our victim outside a concert venue. One of our guys recognized him from a shoplifting arrest a few years ago. We were able to identify the victim from the video and missing posters as well. We only have a circumstantial case because we don't have any sign of them after they left the concert area. But I'll be looking for rentals like you describe as soon as I get back."

"One question, Devon," Smith asked. "My victim had some cut marks on her breasts like you described, but she was strangled and just dumped along the river. There was no overkill like you had with your case."

"Mine either," Morgan said, "as least as far as we know. And if we had a dismemberment, I think we would have heard about that. Some rental owner would have found a lot of blood in their house or something by now."

"Don't know," Anderson said. "We thought that the cuts on the breasts were some kind of punishment for trying to get away, and maybe that's still the case. But it must not be directly connected to the dismemberment, if you have those marks too.

"The only thing I can speculate is that, in our case, the victim somehow escaped and the suspect was probably chasing her around the neighborhood. At one point, for whatever reason, he cut her hand off. Maybe that was enough to get him to go on with dismembering her. I just hope it was something like that, and not that he's escalating his violence."

"One more thing," Morgan said. "In the security video, there is a red-headed woman who kind of looks like she is following Teach and the victim, although she's a ways behind. She was wearing a floppy hat so we couldn't get a good view of her face. But her hair is almost waist-length. A couple of our female officers looked at the tape and both think she's probably in her mid-30's even though we can't make out her face. Does that fit with the woman that was seen at your scene, Devon?"

"We don't have a description of the woman there. A neighbor just thought she had seen a woman in the yard once and that she maybe came in a car. But it makes sense that there was more than one person chasing our victim around the neighborhood.

"A guy across the street says he saw an older Ford or maybe Mercury, blue or black, parked next door to the rental house on one occasion. He just noticed it because he hadn't seen it before but didn't pay that much attention. We think it's probably stolen, but we don't have enough of a description to even put out a BOLO on it. But it's possible it was being driven by the woman, who was staying somewhere else."

The detectives exchanged copies of their case files and agreed to stay in touch. The investigators from Merced and SLO would notify Devon when, and if, they were able to locate a rental house used by Teach.

Now, let's see if our girl went home to Santa Cruz without her parents' knowledge, Anderson thought as he pulled away from the Salinas police building.

Chapter 22

2:55 p.m. — July 12. The 40-mile drive from Salinas to Santa Cruz gave Devon just the right amount of time to mentally go over his plan. Jean Borders had given Angi a list of the addresses of her daughter's friends in the seaside city. In most cases, Jean had also provided parents' names. Devon decided he would start with Casey Logan, the girl identified as Abby's closest friend.

The Logan house was located in an upper-middle class neighborhood. It was an impressive two-story structure, with a columned front porch, more reminiscent of an Old South plantation manor than a trendy resort city home. Devon could almost smell the money and influence.

"May I help you?" a woman in her early 40's asked when she answered Devon's press of the doorbell.

"Yes, ma'am. I'm Detective Devon Anderson from Santa Rosa. I'm investigating a case involving a girl named Abigail Borders and I understand a young lady who lives here is one of her friends. Are you Casey's mother?"

"Yes, I am, Detective. What is this about?"

"May I speak to Casey?" Devon asked, ignoring the woman's query for the moment. "Of course, you may be with her if you wish."

After a pause, the woman stepped back to allow the detective to enter. "Please take a seat in the library, there. I'll get Casey."

"What!? Who is it? A detective?" a male voice boomed from an adjacent room. "I'll talk to him. He's not talking to Casey until I know what this is about!"

"Detective, I'm Josh Logan. I'm Casey's father and an attorney," the man said, his voice calmer now, as he entered the library.

"Nice to meet you, Mr. Logan. I'm Devon Anderson from Santa Rosa."

"I understand you want to talk to my daughter — something about Abby Borders."

Devon nodded.

"I'm afraid I can't permit that until I know what this is about. I'm sure you understand, Detective." Logan motioned Devon to a chair and then sat down facing the investigator.

"Yes, sir. This is the situation. On July 4th, a body was located in Sonoma County. The deceased has been positively identified as Abby. We determined that she was killed in Santa Rosa. Her parents have been notified in Coreyton and it appears that Abby ran away from home up there about a month ago.

"Although we don't know for certain if she came back to Santa Cruz, she had told her parents that was what she wanted to do. Mrs. Borders gave us a list of Abby's friends, with Casey's name at the top of the list. I just want to ask her if she's talked to Abby in the last month."

"Damn, I'm really sorry to hear that. Abby was a great girl. We, my wife and I, like her parents, too. However, I don't think Casey has any information for you. She would have told my wife or me if Abby had contacted her, especially if she knew Abby had run away. I'm sorry, but I don't think you should talk to her."

"I want to, Dad," the teenager said as she burst into the room, tears streaming down her cheeks. "Is she really dead, Detective?"

"Yes, Casey. I'm afraid she is," Devon said.

"Abby was here."

"Casey?" Logan asked.

"I'm sorry, Josh," Mrs. Logan said, following her daughter into the room. "Casey was listening from the hallway."

"Why didn't you tell us, Casey?" Logan asked, nodding his approval for her to join him.

"Because I knew you would report her. She just needed some time to sort out some things, but I guess ..." The teenager broke into sobs.

"It's okay, Casey," Devon said. "No one could have predicted what happened to Abby. Can you tell me about what happened when she came here?"

Casey dabbed her eyes and looked at her father, who nodded for her to continue. "She called me on a Sunday. I think it was the day you and Mom were at the charity auction, Dad."

"That would have been the 16th — June 16th," Mrs. Logan said.

"Yeah, I think so. She called and said she had run away the day before and was at some truck stop up by Fremont. She wanted me to pick her up and bring her here, but I told her I knew Dad would turn her in."

"First, I would have ..." Logan said.

"Shh, Josh. Let her talk," Mrs. Logan said.

"So she asked me to take her to David Calliberry's house. David was kind of her boyfriend last year, but David's dad has a job in Santa Rosa. He had been commuting, but they decided to move up there right after school got out. I thought Abby knew that, but I guess she didn't. So then she asked me to take her to Santa Rosa, but I said I couldn't do that. My parents would have come home before I could get back.

"So I drove her as far as San Francisco and dropped her off downtown where we thought she would be safe. I gave her some money from mom's grocery stash in the kitchen to get a bus ticket to Santa Rosa."

"Grocery stash?" Logan asked.

"Be quiet, Josh. Later."

"Did you hear from her after you dropped her off in San Francisco, Casey?" Devon asked.

"Yeah, she called on Monday evening — the next day."

"You told me that was Cindy Nixon that called," Logan said.

"Josh! Will you just shut up for once!"

Devon nodded to the girl to continue.

"She said she got to Santa Rosa ok, but couldn't find David's address. I guess it's on a new street and she didn't want to ask the cops or anything. She went to the YWCA for the night and then was maybe going to a concert that night, Monday. She thought that might give her a chance to figure out what to do next. There was also a good chance she might spot David at the concert. He goes to every concert he can so it was pretty likely he would be there."

"And that was the last time you heard from her?" Devon asked.

"Yeah. Honest, Dad. I just figured that she either found David and was with him and his parents, or maybe they took her back up to her parents' place in the mountains. I was going to ask her about it when we started school next month, but I didn't really think anymore about it until now."

"Thank you, Casey — Mr. and Mrs. Logan. That's all I need for now." *How much does young Mr. Calliberry know about this? Time to get back to Santa Rosa and ask him.*

Chapter 23

9:15 p.m. — July 12. "Where are we?" Teach mumbled as he woke from a fitful sleep in the back seat of the Mercury. They were descending down a sloping grade on a freeway but Teach recognized neither the highway nor the city ahead.

"Reno," Etta replied from the front seat.

"Reno? I thought you said you wanted to go south."

"I changed my mind. Besides, I thought you might have figured that out when we went through Sacramento! Gawd, you're a dumb-ass."

"OK. So why Reno?"

"Think about it, genius. Nobody knows nobody in this town. Everybody is on the run to somewhere or from somewhere, trying to get rich in the process. Or trying to get lost in the crowd. Not much chance a girl we find here will be looking for friends nearby like the last one was."

"Good thinking, Etta. I guess I'd better find us a house first."

"No, you'd better find *you* a house first."

"I just thought maybe we could stay together this time."

"Don't fuck up a plan that works, dumb shit. You have the phony IDs. I'll get me a motel room just like before, and I'll be around when I want to be. Now, I'll drop you off here. Meet me back here on this corner tomorrow night at 7:00 and you'd better have a house rented by that time."

* * *

Devon didn't really want to work on Saturday, but Christina had taken Holly on a shopping trip to the City. *Damn, Holly is almost 16. Where has the time gone? I need to spend more time with her before she's off to college somewhere.*

Besides, Angi was still technically on administrative leave so she couldn't fulfill her turn as the on-call detective for the weekend. Devon had volunteered to handle any call-outs with the understanding that Angi would cover one of his weekends later. So he wasn't actually free to do whatever he wanted anyway.

It had been nearly 6:00 the night before when Devon arrived back in Santa Rosa, but he took a chance and drove directly to the county clerk's office. One of the clerks was working late and had located a property record for a David Calliberry. *Not too many people around with that name, I'm sure.* The David that he was looking for was too young to own real estate, but it was likely he was David, Jr.

Shortly before 11:00 a.m., Devon parked in front of the newly constructed home. The entire subdivision had been built within the past year and the lots were all sold, although construction continued on many of the homes.

"Mr. Calliberry?" Devon said as he approached a man working in the front yard. "I'm Devon Anderson from the Santa Rosa Police. I'd like to speak to a young David Calliberry. I assume that's your son."

"Yes, sir, it is. Has he done something? He's a good kid."

"No, sir. It's just that he might have some information on a case I'm working on. He's not in any trouble." *Nice to have a concerned father rather than one that wants to 'lawyer up' for his kid right away, even if the lawyer is dad himself.*

"Come on inside, Detective. Too hot to talk out here."

Mrs. Calliberry offered lemonade to her husband and the detective when she learned what was going on, and the four sat around the kitchen table.

"David, do you know Abby Borders?"

"Abby? Sure. We kind of dated off and on last school year but we couldn't really do a lot since we were both only 15. We just sat together at games and met at a couple of dances."

"I understand that your family moved up here from Santa Cruz a month or so ago. Have you heard from Abby since then, or any time since school let out?"

"No, I haven't. Why?"

"Well, Abby ran away from her parents' summer home up in the Sierras and I understand that she might have been trying to find you."

"No. I hadn't even heard that she ran away and I haven't heard from her."

"OK. Thank you. I have to tell you that Abby is dead. She was murdered here in ..."

"Oh, my God!" Mrs. Calliberry said. "Was Abby the girl they found cut up in Lake Sonoma?"

"Yes, ma'am. I'm afraid it was."

"Dave, I saw a picture of the girl in the paper, but I just didn't connect it to Abby. I didn't even think about her being in this town."

David, Jr. looked at his mother, his face a mask of horror. Then tears began to stream down his cheeks. "Detective, are you saying that Abby was in Santa Rosa looking for me, and she got killed because she was here? She got killed because of me?!"

"No, son. Don't think that way. It's not your fault. You didn't even know she would come looking for you, and there's no way you had anything to do with what happened to her," Devon said. *At least, I hope you didn't, but the vibes tell me you're clean on this.*

"No, David," Mr. Calliberry said. "The detective is right. You can't blame yourself for this."

But young David looked at his parents and Detective Anderson, then jumped up from his chair and ran from the room. Devon stood to leave as the parents turned toward the wrenching sound of their son's heart-rending sobs.

Chapter 24

7:42 a.m. — July 15. "Welcome back, stranger. How was the vacation?" Devon asked when Angi walked into the Violent Crimes office.

"Oh, just peachy, Devon. Nothing like a stress interview and a forced vacation while a monster is on the loose to calm your mind," Angi said. "I hope you've been doing more than sitting around here drinking coffee while I've been gone. Gotta keep after you every minute!"

"Yeah, mostly I just sat around and read true detective magazines."

Angi grimaced and flashed her middle finger at Devon.

"But," Devon said, "I was able to get down to Salinas and meet with the guys from Merced and SLO. Neither of them knew about the rented house angle and they're checking on that."

"I doubt they'll have much luck. The perp used a fake ID for the rental. I'm thinking he's done this enough to use a different ID at each location. Unless, of course, some homeowner finds his rental house covered in blood. That might be a clue."

"Don't think there's much chance of that," Devon said, shaking his head. "The body of the girl up in Merced wasn't cut up in any way. She'd been tortured with the same kind of razor cuts. She also had indications of being restrained similar to what youfound in the house here, but she wasn't hacked up.

"As for the girl in SLO, the only thing they have putting Teach with her is a security video. One of their guys had dealt with him before and that's how they ID'd him. They haven't found the girl he was with. One thing though. In the video, it appeared there was a woman with Teach and the girl. She was kind of hanging back, but all three of us felt that she was with them."

"That makes sense. The neighbor, Hammond, thought there had been a woman at the rental house here but didn't have a description of her. What about Santa Cruz?"

"That's where it gets interesting. Abby did go home, as you suspected. She hooked up with a girlfriend but couldn't stay at the girl's house. She wanted to go to a boyfriend's house, but he had moved away."

"Let me guess. To Santa Rosa?"

"That's why you're a detective, Angela," Devon said with a grin. "Yes, but I located the kid and his parents. Abby never made it to his house. The girlfriend dropped her off in San Francisco with fare for a bus. So she could have been taken anywhere between there and here."

"What about bus drivers? Did anyone recognize her?"

"That's next on my list, unless you want to handle it."

"Yeah, I'll do that. I'm anxious to get back to work. Do you know if Jules found out anything about the guy in the lobby?"

Devon blanched. He had been told to let Sergeant Garrison break the news to Angi. But now the question was out there and it was just him and Angi in the office. He couldn't lie to a fellow detective, regardless of instructions from the boss.

"Yeah, she did track down his background. Angi, the guy wasn't involved in the murder. He was sick and ..."

"... And he wanted a cop to end his life for him, because he didn't have the guts to do it himself. What was he? Some kind of drugged up, down on his luck drifter that just ..."

"Angi, no. Sit down."

The defensive mask on Angi's face disappeared.

"His name was William Allen. *Staff Sergeant* William Allen, United States Army. He was suffering from cancer, reportedly caused by exposure to Agent Orange in Vietnam. He was dying and in a lot of pain. It wasn't fair to you, not fair to his family, but you couldn't have known what was really going on with him. You reacted to the situation that was presented to you. No one blames you, including Allen's family."

"But you knew, Devon. Or at least you suspected, right? Is that why you didn't fire?"

"Angi, don't do this to yourself. No, I didn't even suspect that. I didn't fire because ... well, I just didn't. But I thought he was a threat, just like you did. Had I been in front instead of you, then it would have been me on forced days off."

At least, Devon hoped that's the way it would have been. *Would I have fired if I was actually in Angi's position? I don't know. I honestly don't know.*

* * *

"Morning, Devon," Garrison said as he walked into the office forty minutes later. "Have you seen Angi yet?"

"Yeah, she's been here and gone. She's off running down a lead on how the Borders girl may have come to Santa Rosa."

"OK. I really wanted to talk to her but I guess it can wait. Fill me in on what you found out in Salinas and Santa Cruz."

"One thing first, Mike. Angi asked me directly about the ID on the guy in the lobby. I told her what Julie found out."

"Damn! You know I really wanted that to come from me ... but ... but you couldn't lie to her, could you, Devon."

"Not a chance, Boss." *At least not about that. But I did lie to her about why I didn't shoot, at least a little. It was my job to back her up and I ...*

"It's okay, Devon. I'm sure you reassured her that it wasn't her fault — how it all played out. That's what I wanted to make sure she understood."

"She knows, Mike. In her head, she knows. In her gut, well, that will take a little longer."

Chapter 25

9:10 a.m. — July 15. The inter-city bus terminal sat at the edge of the downtown area. It was a dreary place on the outside, but the inside was well lit and clean.

"Hello, sir. I'm Detective Angela Masters. I understand you're the bus line manager here."

"Yes, ma'am. I'm Arlie Fritz. What can I do for you?"

"I'm trying to determine if a teen-aged girl caught a bus from somewhere in downtown San Francisco and got off here."

"Sure. Let's go to my office. Do you have a name? Was this yesterday?"

"Her name was Abigail Borders. And this would have been about a month ago."

"Whew. That makes it a little tougher. But I can check the charge slips."

"Most likely, she paid cash."

"Well, in that case, she wouldn't even have had to give her name. That's a tall order, Detective."

"I know, but it's really important. The girl was murdered here in ..."

"The girl from up at the lake? That girl?!"

"Yes, sir."

"Runaway, right? And now her family has to deal with not only her loss, but the way she died?"

"Yes, sir. That's why I need all the help I can get to find out exactly where she was abducted. I'm hoping that will give me a lead to find whoever killed her."

"You'll have my complete cooperation, Detective. Let me tell you something. Eighteen years ago, my daughter was murdered in an alley outside her apartment. She was a sophomore at UC-Berkeley and the first person in our family to attend college. She was my life." Fritz stared at the wall over Angi's shoulder.

After a moment, he shook his head to regain his composure. "But thanks to a guy who came forward with some key information, the guy who killed her is doing life. It won't bring her back but … Anyway, knowing that the cops got him helped give us some closure. If I can help this family get the same thing, then it's the least I can do.

"Last bus from the San Francisco run gets in at 8:00 p.m. There are three drivers on that route. Come back a little before eight, and I'll have them all here. You can ask them yourself."

* * *

Etta had cruised past the downtown intersection at least 20 times in the past two days, but Teach was nowhere to be seen. *I'm gonna kill that little shit …*

Suddenly, a small man with a dense black beard, wearing a Navy pea coat and a slouch hat, ran into the street from a recessed doorway. Etta swerved the Mercury to keep from hitting him.

"Get in, asshole!" she said. "What part of 'meet me at 7:00 p.m. on Saturday night' didn't you understand? You do know it's almost noon on *Monday*?"

"I'm sorry, Etta. It took me a while to find a place. But you'll like it. You really will!"

"OK, where is this place?"

"Take the main road out of town toward the south. There's a big valley out there between here and Carson City. I found a perfect place on a side road in the valley. Hardly any houses around at all."

Thirty minutes later, following Teach's directions, Etta turned at a sign labeled *Franktown Rd.* It was a winding two lane road off Highway 395, the main thoroughfare through the Washoe Valley.

"How in the hell did you get way out here?" Etta asked. "You didn't have a car."

"I bummed a ride from a guy I met in a bar. Don't worry. I gave him a hundred bucks to not remember anything. Turn in here."

"Shit. What are all those boulders all over the place? This place looks abandoned and ..."

"Yeah, it is. That's the beauty of it. The guy in the bar told me that a couple of years ago, the whole side of the mountain slid away. There was mud and rocks and shit all over this area. A lot of houses like this one — even some big mansion places — got wiped out by the mud. The owners of this place just gave up and moved away."

"Well, at least you didn't have to use up an ID to rent this dump. But remember, you have to live in it and I'm guessing there's no air conditioner."

"No power, but we can get some lanterns. And the place has a basement. The people left behind a couple of mattresses in a bedroom upstairs. There was also some rope and a little logging chain on a workbench in the basement. I already pulled one of the mattresses down there so there's everything we need. Now, we just have to find a girl."

* * *

Angi returned to the bus station at 7:45. "Gentlemen, thank you for being here," Angi said. "I know from Mr. Fritz that at least one of you has been off for several hours, and I appreciate you coming back in. I know what I'm asking is a stretch. Each of you sees hundreds of people each day, and I'm talking about something that happened nearly a month ago. But if you will take a look at this picture, and let me know if you recognize this girl."

Angi passed a photo of Abby that her father had given her. "Her name was Abigail Borders and she was murdered. But we have reason to believe that she caught a bus from somewhere in downtown San Francisco to Santa Rosa sometime around the 16th or 17th of last month."

Each driver in turn looked at the photo and shook his head.

"Thank you, gentlemen. I knew it was a long shot, but ..."

"Detective, are you sure one of us picked her up in San Francisco?" one driver asked.

"No, I'm not sure of that. Why?"

The driver looked warily at Fritz. "Well, I ..."

"It don't matter, Jim. If you seen this girl, you tell. Don't matter how she got on your bus."

"Well," Jim said, "I think I picked her up but it wasn't in San Francisco. She was walking along Highway 101, down near Corte Madera, and thumbed me down. We ain't supposed to pick up anyone except at designated bus stops, but ..." He looked at Fritz.

"Go ahead, Jim. I ain't your boss right now. I'm just a man who wants to help this detective find the guy who killed this little girl. Ain't nobody here gonna say nothing about no piddly-assed policy violation."

"She just looked so cold, even though it was a June evening. And lonely — God, she looked so cold and lonely." Jim gazed blankly at the wall. "So I picked her up. I didn't even charge her for the ride."

"And did you bring her here to the station?"

"No. I dropped her off right by the YWCA. I told her she could probably get a cheap place to stay there and it would be safe. That's the last I saw of her."

Chapter 26

8:30 p.m. — July 17. Miranda Arellano huddled in a doorway on Virginia Street. Two blocks away, a neon arch spanned the street, flashing its iconic message: *Reno - The Biggest Little City in the World.*

From the doorway, the 15-year-old watched the throngs of people move past. A few were laughing, backslapping and boasting of their good fortune at winning in a casino. Most were blank-faced, moving along the sidewalks like people everywhere do. A few were glum, their modest finances left behind at a roulette table or slot machine. But happy or sad, no one noticed Miranda.

It seemed to Miranda that no one ever noticed her. She was from a poor family that lived on the outskirts of Fernley, Nevada. In school, Miranda was an average student but had few friends. Her family's financial situation did not permit her to join into the social structure of the school and she was perceived as an outsider.

Galen was different. He, too, was from a poor family, but his family lived in town. He was also blessed with a natural ability on the basketball court. That gave him an in with some of the guys, but the girls still shunned him, according to the unwritten pecking order of the high school. He — alone it seemed to her — saw Miranda's inner beauty and they became a couple.

But now, in the summer, neither teenager was invited into the activities of their school peers.

"We should just get out of here," Galen told Miranda one day. "I could take us to Reno, or maybe even San Francisco. Nobody would look down on us there."

Three days later, at 2:00 a.m., Miranda slipped out the back door of her small house and ran a quarter mile down the dirt driveway to where Galen waited in his battered Chevy pickup. The great adventure began.

But within two days, the adventure had soured. Neither teenager had much money, and what they had disappeared quickly with the need to buy food and gas. They slept in the pickup but still, money was a major problem.

"I'm going home," Galen said on the third day of the adventure. "I've got enough gas to get back and that's about it. I can't do this anymore." The boy knew he would face harsh punishment from his father when he returned but he didn't know what else to do. "Come on, Miranda, let's go home."

"I can't, Galen. My father will kill me. And if he doesn't, my brother will. They'll disown me and I'll be on the street anyway, so I might as well stay here."

"Come on, Miranda. It's not that bad. I know your brother and I know he's missing you. And I'm sure your dad is, too. Let's go back."

But in the end, Miranda stayed in Reno. Now, nearly a week since she fled down her driveway, excited about a life with Galen in the city, she sat alone in the doorway. Her stomach protested, but with less than a dollar in the pocket of her ragged jeans, she had no idea how she was going to get another meal.

"You ok, honey?" a woman asked. Miranda slowly raised her head to see a hard-looking woman, maybe 40 years old, standing in front of her.

Miranda nodded, but her eyes betrayed her. She was far from okay.

But was this woman her savior? The first thing she noticed was the woman's red hair — huge, permed-to-death hair, crimped and stiff with hairspray. The woman wore a cut-up sweatshirt with one shoulder hanging off, a black bra showing through cut-out holes in the shirt. Her high-waisted, acid-washed jeans fit snugly on her legs. Miranda's eyes traced the jeans down to the ragged hems and the woman's feet. Her dirty, crowded toes popped out the ends of her high-heeled Candies shoes.

"Come on now, sweetie. I can see you're in a tough fix. Let me help you. How long since you ate?"

"A while," Miranda lied. It had been nearly 30 hours.

The woman led Miranda to a nearby casino and plunked down $6.95 for the 'all you can eat' buffet. "Help yourself, honey. All you want. Go ahead now."

Wow, if Galen had known we could get this much food for $6.95, he might have stuck around for a couple more days and maybe we could have made it. We were spending that much on just a hamburger and fries and a Coke at the drive-ins.

An hour later, Miranda found the woman waiting for her at the entrance to the buffet.

"Feel better, honey?"

"Yes, ma'am. Thank you." In reality, Miranda was actually feeling ill. Not only was the buffet 'all you can eat' but there were trays of food she had never tried: Shrimp and calimari and crab legs. Mangos and pineapples. Veal and lamb. The girl's system was accustomed to a more egalitarian diet, and the exotic foods played havoc with her bowels.

"Come on. I'll bet you don't have a place for your head tonight. You can come to my house."

Miranda thought about protesting, but the woman had been so nice to her so far. Besides, she couldn't spend another night sleeping in a dirty doorway.

* * *

It was dark outside and the car was no longer in the city when Miranda awoke with a start. *Where am I? This isn't Fernley.* Then the memory of the last few days began to return. The lonely street, the kindly woman. But ...

"Alright, honey. Get your pretty little ass out of the car!" The voice came from the woman who had been so kind to her, but the woman's face was now a mask of menace and contempt.

"She said get out of the fucking car, you little bitch!" A man's hand grabbed Miranda's arm and jerked her body from the front seat of the car. The force was so great that she crashed to the ground, landing in some kind of fine dust mixed with large rocks. From the ground, all she could see was the clear sky and the outlines of gigantic boulders strewn across the area.

The man jerked her up by her arm and with his other hand twisted a large quantity of her hair into his fist. He pulled her face close to his. His wild, curly beard scraped her cheek and the stench of cigarettes and beer from his mouth assaulted her nose. "Move it!"

"Help me!" Miranda screamed.

"Shut it, honey. Nobody can hear you out here." The woman seemed even more menacing than the man now, if that were possible.

Miranda was shoved into a dark house, its filthy interior illuminated by a single camp lantern. As the man propelled her down a flight of stairs, the woman followed, carrying the lantern.

The man shoved Miranda roughly onto a dust-covered mattress on the floor in a corner of the basement. Then she felt something metal being clasped around her ankle and the sound of a padlock closing.

"Get some sleep, honey," the woman laughed. "You'll need some stamina for what we have in mind for you later."

Chapter 27

10:40 a.m. — July 19. "Sorry it took so long to get this footage, Detective," the manager of the Luther Center said. "I wasn't even sure we would still have it, since we recycle our security tapes after a month."

Twenty minutes later, Kim had the VHS tape cued up on the player in the lab. "I'll take a run-through and let you know what I find," she told Angi.

Three hours later, Angi was at her desk when the phone rang. "Detectives, Masters," she answered in her customary way. "May I .."

"Got her, Angi!" Kim's voice said.

"Be right there!"

"I'm pretty sure this is Abby," Kim said, pointing at the frozen image on the TV screen. "But this is the only shot I have that I think might be her, and she's with a woman. I haven't seen anyone that looks like Teach to me."

"Can you get a picture of that screen for me?"

* * *

An hour later, Sergeant Garrison assembled Devon, Kim, Angi, and Julie Phelps in the small violent crimes conference room. Kim brought a cart holding a VHS player and television which barely fit into the room with the detectives gathered.

"Thanks for making the time for this," Angi said to the investigators. "This is the security tape from the entrance to the

Luther Center on the evening that our victim, Abby Borders, told her friend that she was attending a concert. We think she was trying to meet a boy she knew from her hometown, but he didn't know she was coming and didn't attend the concert that night.

"Kim has gone through the tape and couldn't ID anyone as our suspect, Edward Teach. However, she did isolate this shot of a girl that we are pretty sure is Abby. As you can see, she's with a woman."

"Looks to me like she's with the woman voluntarily," Devon said. "I don't see the woman holding on to her, by the arm or whatever. Looks to me like they are just walking together."

"And the rest of the shot of them, only about four seconds, bears that out," Kim said.

"We have information from a neighbor next door to the house where we're sure Abby was killed that a woman showed up there on two or three occasions," Angi said. "I'm thinking that maybe this woman is an accomplice. She gets the girls for Teach — somehow persuades them to go along with her voluntarily until Teach takes control of them. By then, they are captives."

"That makes a lot of sense, Angi," Garrison said. "Any way to identify this woman?"

"There's nothing I could see that would ID her," Kim said. "She and Abby are only in the frame for a few seconds. Even the closest parking is quite a ways away. Only the main parking lot has security cameras. The tapes from those have all been recycled, so we don't have her getting into a car."

"And given the amount of time that's passed, I doubt we'd find anyone who would remember them, unless there was a struggle of some type. But then, I would think we would have heard about that already," Julie added.

"I have an idea, Boss," Angi said. "It's a long shot, but ... I'll be back in a while."

"And she's off," Devon quipped.

* * *

"Mr. Detwiler, I need your help again," Angi said as she walked through the door of the Detwiler Property Management office.

"Of course, Detective ... Masters, wasn't it?"

"Yes. Remember, we were talking about the rental house, the one your records showed as being rented by a guy named Parker?"

"Yes, I remember. The cashier's check he used to pay me turned out to be a forgery, but I suppose you know that."

"Yes, sir. Is there anything else you remember about him?"

"No, not really. I can tell you that the owners were really upset. It cost them a bundle to have their house cleaned up, plus they lost out on the rent because of the phony payment. But they took my suggestions and tightened up the rental process ..."

"That's great, Mr. Detwiler. Now, about Parker. Was there anyone with him when he first rented the house? A woman, maybe."

"No, no. I'm pretty sure he was alone. Just walked in here and ... I have to tell you, I would have been more comfortable if there had been a woman with him. He was pretty scary."

"What about a car? Did you happen to see his car?"

"Car? No, I don't think so. He walked ... wait! Yeah, yeah, yeah. I have it here somewhere!"

Angi's inquisitive look was obvious as the startled little man bolted toward the file cabinets in the back of the office.

"Yes. Yes. Yes! Here it is! I told you the guy was pretty scary, so when he left, I got up and kind of looked out the window to be sure he was gone. He got into a '79 or '80 Mercury Cougar. I always wanted one of those, but this one was black. I don't like black cars."

"Did you happen to get the license number, Mr. Detwiler?"

"Yep, sure did. Wrote it right here on the back of the contract. I didn't put it on the front because the owners didn't ..."

"Thank you, Mr. Detwiler," Angi said as she wrote the number in her notebook.

"One more thing, Detective."

"Yes?" *I need to get on this and don't really need to hear more about how much you love cars.*

"There was a woman, a red-head. Rough looking if you know what I mean. She was driving the car."

Chapter 28

11:30 a.m. — July 19. "Dispatch, Washoe 3011," the Washoe County Sheriff's Deputy said into his radio microphone. "I'm here with the complainant. We're just inside the entrance to Davis Creek Park. I need one more unit and a supervisor to my location."

"OK, sir. Please tell my sergeant and Deputy Olsen what you told me," the deputy said when the other two law officers arrived.

"Like I was telling Deputy Charters here, I've been noticing what looks like somebody down at the old Stillwell place. It's just up the road there, not quite to Bowers Mansion. The Stillwell's house got hit directly by the muck from Slide Mountain and they wound up moving into Carson City. Their place is abandoned, just waiting on the insurance to decide on a final settlement. But the last few nights, I've been seeing lights in the house. A couple of times, there has been a car there, too."

"Could it have just been the Stillwells? Maybe they came back to get some stuff out of the house," the sergeant asked.

"No. I called Marty Stillwell and he said they got everything they could out already. He said they haven't been back out here since a week or two after the slide. Eloise — that's Mrs. Stillwell — can't bear to look at the place, so even if they have to go to Reno, they never get off of 395."

"No car there now, Sarge. I checked again while we were waiting for you. But there are fresh tire tracks in the dirt on the driveway," Deputy Charters said.

"Marty said he wants you to check it out, Sergeant. He still owns the place until the insurance settles and he's afraid of vandalism that might hurt the settlement."

"OK, guys. Let's take a look."

* * *

"Definitely been someone here, Sarge," Charters said as the three entered the abandoned house.

"Be careful, guys. Who knows how unstable this place might be after being hit with a hundred tons of mud and rocks?"

"Got some food and beer in an ice chest here. And a bunch of empty beer bottles tossed in the corner."

"I didn't see anything in the rest of the house. No lights or water, of course, but someone recently took a shit in ... What was that?"

"Got something, Bob?"

"I thought I heard something under the floor. Is there a basement to this place?"

"Yeah. Over there. That looks like a door to either a closet or a basement. I'm surprised this place is still sitting on a basement, as much as the upper part is leaning."

"Door's locked, Sarge. With a new padlock!"

"Break it down!"

Charters put his weight behind a kick and the door flew open. Wood splinters and the dislodged padlock and hasp crashed down the wooden stairs.

"No. *Please!* Please don't hurt me anymore!" a female voice sniffled from the darkness.

"Check it out, guys!" the supervisor said as he reached for the portable radio on his belt. "Dispatch, Washoe 3010. Get an ambulance headed to my location, code three!"

"Over here!" Olsen said as the beam from his four-cell flashlight splayed across the pitch black cast of the basement. "There's a girl over here!"

The young woman sat on a filthy mattress in a back corner of the basement. She tried to cover her naked body as two flashlight beams played around her. Despite her efforts, the deputies could see large welts on her bare legs and back.

"We're sheriff's deputies, miss. You're safe now!" Charters said. "Can you get up?"

"No, she can't," Olsen said, as he played his flashlight beam down the rusty chain attached to the girl's left leg. The chain was padlocked to her leg so tightly that the links cut into her flesh. Another padlock fastened the opposite end of the short chain around a sewer pipe.

"Here!" Charters said, spying a rusted axe on a workbench a few feet away. "Smash that fucking thing off that pipe and let's get her out of here!"

The sergeant had grabbed a blanket from the trunk of his patrol car. He came down the stairs just as the deputies were helping the girl to stand.

"What's your name, miss?" he asked as he wrapped the blanket around her.

"Miranda ... Miranda Arellano."

"The girl missing from Fernley?" Charters asked.

Miranda nodded and then buried her head on Charters' chest, rivulets of salty tears cutting canyons through the fine dust on her cheeks.

"You're safe now, Miranda. We won't let anything else happen to you."

As the three deputies helped the young girl out of the littered house, an ambulance pulled into the dirt crusted driveway.

And a black Mercury cruised slowly by, before accelerating south on Franktown Road toward Carson City.

* * *

"Mr. Arellano, your daughter has been found and she's safe," the Lyon County deputy told the man who answered his knock on the weathered door.

"Thank you, Deputy. Thank you. Is she ok? Is she hurt?"

"I'm told she's been hurt but is in the Reno Medical Center. It's one of the best facilities in the country, so she's being well cared for."

"Has she been in Reno the whole time? The parents of the boy who drove her to Reno called us after he came back without her. They said she wouldn't come back with him. I drove over there and walked around the streets for hours, showing people her picture, but I couldn't find her. Nobody would say they saw her."

"I don't know the answer to that, sir. A Washoe County deputy will meet you at the hospital to fill you in on what's happened. We can talk more later, if you need to. For now, take your family and see your daughter. I'm sure she wants to see you."

Chapter 29

2:35 p.m. — July 19. "What's the verdict, Doc?" Detective Al Lawrence asked. The Washoe County investigator had seen his share of victimized runaways. He and his Reno PD counterparts worked tirelessly to identify runaways and get them off the streets. It was a daunting task because there seemed to be more of them, mostly young girls, every year. Fortunately, most of them didn't suffer to the extent that Miranda had.

"Well, it's not pretty. She's been raped, several times. Then there's the bruising. Looks to me like she was beaten with some hard, flat object, maybe a board. There are also rope marks on her neck and upper torso. Appears that she was tied to some object, maybe a pole or something upright, with a rope around her neck and another immobilizing her upper arms."

"And the leg restraint?"

"Yes, but I think that was separate. From what the deputies told me, she was chained to a sewer pipe. That was probably just to keep her from escaping while the suspect was gone. I think the rope binding was used to hold her while she was tortured."

"Tortured? Like being beaten with a board?"

"Well, yes, that, but something else. Damnedest thing I've ever seen. She has tiny cuts on the underside of both breasts. It looks like someone immobilized her then lifted her breasts and just made little slits an inch or so long in various directions on the underside. Painful as hell, probably, but not life threatening. The implement was thin and sharp, probably a razor blade or maybe a hobby knife."

"Shit! I remember seeing a teletype from someplace in California. Runaway girl was killed and she had cuts just like you describe."

"Well, Detective, I can't tell you anything more, but I hope you can get this son-of-a-bitch, and soon."

"Can I talk to her, Doc?"

"You know I can't let you talk to her until the parents give the okay, as long as she's in the hospital's care. But medically, she's ok. Psychologically, it might be a different story. But as soon as the parents get here and I talk to them about her condition, I'll let you know so you can get their okay to talk to her."

* * *

"Detectives, Masters," Angi answered the phone in her usual way.

"Angi, this is dispatch. We have a transfer call for you from a Detective Lawrence in Reno. Sounds like your guy has struck again."

"Is she alive?" Angi asked the moment the call was connected.

"Yes, she is. Who am I speaking to?"

"Sorry. This is Detective Angela Masters. Detective Lawrence, right?"

"Yes. Call me Al. We have a 15-year-old runaway that was found in an abandoned house in the county south of Reno. She's been raped and has cuts on her breasts like your teletype described. But she's alive and doing okay under the circumstances."

"And you got to her before she was murdered? Do you have Teach in custody?"

119

"Teach? Is that your suspect?"

"Yes. Edward Lloyd Teach."

"Interesting name. Sorry but we don't have anyone in custody, and so far we don't have any leads on the suspect. Our deputies responded to a trespassing call at an abandoned house and found her chained up in the basement. But I haven't been able to talk to her yet and we haven't finished processing the scene."

"Do you think she'll be able to talk anytime soon?"

"Yes. The doctor says she's okay medically to talk. However, since she's a minor, I have to get permission from at least one parent. The parents are on their way. They are only about 40 miles away, so I suspect they should be here within the next half-hour."

"Of course, I can't ask you to hold off on your questioning, but I'm going to drive over. It's four – four and a half hours, give or take, but I'd like to see where she was being held and your evidence for myself."

* * *

It was just after 7:00 p.m. when Angi drove into the parking lot of the sheriff's office on the north side of Reno. "Thanks for waiting for me, Al," she said when she had been directed to Lawrence's desk.

"Angela? Good to meet you. I had a chance to talk to Miranda, the victim. I can brief you on what she said, but I think we should head out for the scene if you want to look at it while it's still daylight. It's about 20 miles south of here."

"Please, call me Angi," she said when they were in Lawrence's car. "So what did your victim have to say?"

"Well, as I think I already told you, she was a runaway. Thought she could solve her problems on the streets of the city. She had been in Reno for several days — four or five, maybe a week. She's a little fuzzy on that. She was hanging out downtown when a woman approached her. The woman bought her some food and then told her she was going to take her to her home."

"Well, that makes sense. We have info that a woman was involved in our case, but we haven't identified her. We do have a video of our victim at a concert, accompanied by a woman."

"Uh huh. So, the girl fell asleep and when she woke up, they were at a dark house out in the country somewhere. That's all she could tell me. There was a man there, who pushed her downstairs and chained her to a pipe.

"Over the next few days — she isn't sure how long, but our timeline says about three days — she was stripped and left naked all the time. She said the man was there almost all the time, but when the woman would come around, that's when it got bad."

"Really?"

"The woman would order the guy to tie her up, and then the woman would scream and curse at her. She also hit the girl with a one-by-four that was in the basement. She's pretty bruised up from that."

"And the cuts?"

"The woman did that to her, too. She said the guy never participated in any of that. Now, the guy did rape her, but only when the woman wasn't there. She said the guy was not as rough with her, although he was raping her. But when the woman came around, the guy just stood back and didn't do anything unless the woman told him to."

"That's a new twist. I certainly didn't expect to hear that."

"And here's the real shocker for me. The girl was raped — she thinks four or five times — by the woman, wearing a strap-on. And she said the woman was brutal."

Chapter 30

8:19 a.m. — July 22. "It was our guy, Mike." Angi was briefing her supervisor on her trip to Reno. "The deputies found his prints on a camp lantern that was in the house as well as on several beer bottles. The victim told them that a woman was also involved, but they didn't find any prints or anything else tying a woman to the scene."

"What about the plate number you got from the rental place?"

"It comes back on a black '79 Mercury Cougar, just like the guy said. Registered owner is a Henrietta L. Place with an address in Alturas. I put in a call to the Modoc County SO to check it out, but I haven't heard back from them yet."

At that moment, a records clerk knocked on the doorframe of Garrison's office. "Here's the print-out you asked for, Detective," she said as she handed a single piece of paper to Angi.

"Henrietta Lucinda Place. Born 12-12-1952. Arrests for prostitution in San Francisco and Oakland back in '80 and '81. Served six months in Alameda County. No record since."

"So now she's hooked up with this Teach character and she's being the front man to get young girls for him. He rapes and tortures them, then kills them and moves on."

"Close, Mike, but it might be kind of the other way around. The victim in Reno told the detective that the woman, presumably Place, was the main aggressor. She was the one who did the torturing. The guy raped the girl, but the woman did too, and was far more brutal about it."

"And I thought I'd heard about everything. What about links to Merced or San Luis Obispo?"

"Devon called the two detectives there on Friday. They haven't been able to locate any rental properties that they can tie to Teach. And SLO still hasn't turned up their victim, or her body."

"Angi," Julie said from the doorway. "Call for you. It's Modoc County."

* * *

"Deputy Sylvester," Julie said as she transferred the call to Angi's line.

"Whatcha got, deputy?"

"Well, your Ms. Place has quite a history. I'm kind of new, so I never heard of her. But when I mentioned her name to the sheriff, he knew all about her."

"Does she still live there, or have family there?"

"No, neither. In fact, the address you gave me was right for the place she grew up in, but it's been torn down for years. There's an auto parts store there now."

But her car registration is current to that address. Someone didn't check very well, Angi thought. "So what can you tell me about her, Deputy Sylvester?"

"This is mostly from the sheriff's recollection, but here's what we have. Etta — she goes by Etta — apparently moved here with her brother when she was little. The sheriff thinks it was about the time he first started on the department, so something like 30-32 years ago.

"She had a brother who was a couple of years older. The kids came here to live with their grandmother after their father was murdered in prison. After the father's death, the mother just left them in the waiting room of the hospital in Klamath Falls, Oregon. Etta had a note pinned to her dress with the grandmother's address."

"Rough way to start life."

"Yeah. So she had a fairly normal childhood, I guess. Sheriff said she wasn't in trouble in school. Average student. Nothing outstanding. Then when she was 14, she got pregnant. Caused quite a stir around here when she claimed that her brother had raped her and that he was the father."

"Yeah, that would probably stir things up in most towns! What happened to the baby?"

"She gave it up for adoption in Redding and then ran away. The grandmother died a year or so later, and the brother lit out right after that. No one's seen Etta or her brother since."

"So she's been living on her own since she was 15, 16?"

"Yep. The sheriff says he heard from a girl she went to school with that she took up with another woman and they were living together, but the girl didn't know where or the sheriff couldn't remember. Anyway, that was ten or twelve years ago. Nothing since then at all."

"OK, thanks. Let the sheriff know, just for his information, that she was arrested for prostitution in San Francisco and Oakland a few years ago. She did a couple of months in county but that's the last we have on her until she turned up in the case I told you about."

"Thanks, Detective. I'll be sure to call you if we hear anything about her."

Little likelihood of that, Angi thought as she hung up the phone. *I think Etta Place has moved far beyond the placid lifestyle of Alturas, California — and not in a good way.*

* * *

"And that sums up what we know now," Angi said after briefing Sergeant Garrison on the call from Modoc County. "Frankly, I have more questions than answers. Teach sounds on paper like the badass, but the girl in Reno says it's the other way around. Yet, Teach is the one left with the victims. Teach used a good-quality phony ID to rent the house here that they used to hold Abby. But Place seems to stay somewhere else, and drives her own car. I presume it was the same in the other locations, except that they found an abandoned house in Reno instead of renting one.

"Finally, there's the issue of why they butchered Abby. The girl in Merced was tortured in the same way and raped, but she was just murdered. And there was no indicator that they planned to dismember the girl in Reno. So what caused Teach to go off here?"

"And are you sure it was Teach that butchered her, Angi?"

"Come on, Mike. That's a little much for a woman, don't you think?"

"One hunch panned out, Angi," Julie said from the door. "I just got off the phone with the manager of the Bacchus Inn. Place stayed there during the whole time that Teach was in the rental house. The guy remembered the wild red hair."

"And how did you figure out to call there?" Garrison asked.

"Superior investigative ability, Sarge," Julie grinned.

"Yeah, Mike. That, and I had Hagen's rookie officer sit down at a desk last Saturday and call every motel and hotel in Sonoma County until we found the right place," Angi said, straight-faced. "Now I just need to call the other agencies and have them do the same."

Little could she know that it would be many weeks before any of her questions would be answered.

Chapter 31

10:53 a.m. — August 12. "I ain't seen the ole boy in 'bout a week," Tom Cavendish, the proprietor of the Cali-Ho Hotel told the responding officers. His yellow teeth were barely visible through his ungroomed whiskers. "So I took my passkey and went to check on him. He's in there, in his room, but there's a chain on the door. He's on the bed, awful still, but I wasn't sure what I should do. So I called y'all."

The Cali-Ho Hotel was, in reality, a flop house inhabited by the dregs of the city. Located above a hardware store in downtown Santa Rosa, the place rented rooms by the week. There was no elevator, no maid service, no linen service, or much of any other kind of service. But for $27 a week, the residents couldn't expect much. It was one step above sleeping under an overpass, although it was a short step since the overpass might have been cleaner.

"OK, let's take a look," Jared Hagen told the prop. Hagen and Probationary Officer Eric Miller followed Cavendish down a grimy hallway. At least it felt grimy to Hagen. It was hard to tell with only two bare light bulbs lighting the forty foot long passageway.

The hallway was barely four feet wide. Mounds of trash along the walls reduced the available walking space to less than half that. As least three rats, each about the size of a dachshund, Miller was certain, scurried for cover as the men padded along the cracked linoleum.

"Right here, number five," Cavendish said. Before he even entered the room, Hagen could smell the putrid odor of decomposition. He took the passkey from Cavendish and turned the deadbolt. The inside chain lock was indeed in place, but it didn't stop a billowing stench of decomp from roiling through the three inch opening of the door.

"God, man. You didn't smell that?" Hagen looked at Cavendish. Miller, on his first dead body call, fought to keep his lunch down as the pungent odor assaulted his nostrils.

"Well, yeah, I did," Cavendish replied, "but some of these people ain't too neat. You should see the shit I have to clean out of some of these rooms when somebody moves out."

"Well, that ain't the smell of shit, mister," Hagen snarled as he reared back and kicked the door open, splinters of the frame flying from where the chain lock gave way.

The man, Ned Low, according to Cavendish, lay on his back on the sagging double bed, which was covered with neither sheets nor a blanket. A single low wattage bulb marginally lit the room. Low was dressed in a dirty white sleeveless undershirt and khaki pants. He wore no socks. A pair of worn boots lay haphazardly by the bed. The man had obviously been there for some time.

To add to the gut-wrenching stench, the room was oppressively hot. An ancient steam radiator churned the putrid air. The single window in the room, which overlooked the alley behind the hardware store, was closed and locked.

"Let's get some air in here," Hagen said to Miller, jerking his head toward the window. "I'll call it in."

Miller flipped the thumb latch on the double-hung window, and lifted the bottom section. It stopped abruptly after about eight inches and would not budge. A stub of dowel had been glued into each side of the window frame, prohibiting the window from opening higher.

He looked at Cavendish, who merely shrugged and murmured, "Keeps 'em from skipping out the back."

"You know that's a fire code violation!" Hagen said.

"Mac, this whole damn place is one big fire code violation."

Hagen couldn't disagree with the greasy-haired proprietor. Without a word to the prop, he walked to the front desk and dialed an unpublished number.

"Detectives, Masters," the answering voice said.

"Angi, this is Jared Hagen. We have a DB over in the Cali-Ho. Looks like a natural but do you want to take a look before I call the coroner?"

"OK, I'll take a walk down. Just keep the place contained."

Masters made an unrushed five block walk from the detective offices to the Cali-Ho. The scene was under control and, besides, if Jared Hagen thought the death was due to natural causes, he was most likely correct. Calling a detective to the scene was almost a formality.

Cavendish had returned to the front desk, where he met Masters. He sullenly told the detective which room contained the body, making no effort to show her the way or to provide any information.

What a sleaze ball, Angi thought. "Whatcha got, Jared?" she asked as she walked into the room. "My God! It's hot in here."

"Yeah. You should have been here twenty minutes ago. We closed the radiator valve, which was wide open, and tried to open a window. But as you can see, it will only go up part way."

The open doorway provided a little cross breeze. In most hotels, the officers would have closed the door, trying to keep the decomp gases from permeating the hallways. But in the Cali-Ho, sadly, it merely blended into the ambiance of the dump.

"Angi, meet Ned Low. We don't know much about him except that he's lived here for about three months. Pays his rent on time but apparently doesn't have a job or any family that the prop knows of. The prop says he gave the guy a break on the room because he was a former sailor.

"I ran his name in the system. He's had a couple of petty beefs, theft and running out on a food bill. He served a couple of months in Yolo County for that, but otherwise, he looks clean.

"The room was completely locked from the inside when we got here. As you can see, I kicked the door to get past the chain lock. The window was also locked from the inside. I didn't see any signs of injury. Looks like the old guy just lay down on the bed and died."

"OK, go ahead and call the coroner," Angi said. "I'll just take a quick look."

Angi looked closely at the body of the old man on the bed. At first, she saw nothing which caused her any concern. She was about to notify Hagen that she concurred with his assessment when the light coming through the hazy window splayed across the dead man's chest.

Angi bent over, looking closely at the man's shirt, its once white luster now dulled by a combination of sweat, dirt and the stains of at least three different food groups.

"Jared, hand me your flashlight. I'm not sure but I thought I saw a little reflection from a spot on the shirt front."

Angi carefully panned the light beam across the shirt front at a low angle. "Guys, I got something. Help me lift this guy's shirt."

"What is it, Detective?" Miller asked as they slid the shirt upward.

"It was only a pinhole sized stain. I would have missed it too if the light hadn't caught it just right. But the stain is blood … and that's a bullet hole – in the guy's chest!"

Chapter 32

11:36 a.m. — August 12. "OK, guys, let's find the gun. Jared, you said the room was completely sealed?"

"Like a drum … a very hot drum."

"Maybe he's laying on it," Miller said.

"Most likely," Angi replied. When the officers were certain no gun was laying openly on the bed, Angi said, "OK, let's roll him up on his left side and see if it's underneath him."

No luck.

"OK, Jared. Let's call the lab and have one of the techs run a couple of lights down here. We need to see what we're doing in here."

Ten minutes later, a lab technician arrived with two high-power halogen lights mounted on tripod poles. The lights were normally used to light a crime scene at night.

"I think one will do it," Angi said. "Anybody see an outlet to plug this in?"

The single outlet in the room produced no power.

"Get that proprietor up here," Angi said, her irritation growing.

"Yeah, all the plugs on this side of the hall are out. Keep blowing fuses. Nobody seems to mind, though," Cavendish said.

"Well, Mr. Cavendish, why don't you take Aaron here and find one that works. We'll run an extension cord if we have to."

Another five minutes passed before the halogen bulb glowed to life. Under the intense illumination, the meager contents of the room were now readily apparent. Beside the double bed where the deceased man lay, there was a rickety plastic nightstand. A worn four-drawer pressed-board chest of drawers occupied the far corner, a single burner electric hot plate resting on its top. A door in the wall opposite the bed led to a tiny closet.

"Son-of-a-bitch!" Cavendish growled as he peered from the hallway into the room at the illegal, by hotel rules, hot plate. "No wonder the fuses kept blowing! He was cooking in his room. I should dangle that shithead off the roof by his big toes to teach him a les…"

"Yeah, I can see you run a tight ship here," Angi said. "But it's a little late for that."

"Oh, yeah … sorry."

"Please go back downstairs, Mr. Cavendish. We'll call you if we need you."

"Where's the bathroom?" Miller asked, as he eyed the claustrophobic room.

"Down the hall, sonny," Cavendish called over his shoulder. "This ain't the Hilton."

On knees and latex-gloved hands, the officers searched the room closest to the body, under the bed and in the night stand. They found no gun, nor did they locate any shell casings.

"OK, guys. Check the chest of drawers over there and the closet. See if there's maybe an attic access in the closet where someone could have slipped out," Angi said. "There has to be a reasonable explanation for this."

Hagen searched the rickety chest. It contained two shirts, one pair of khaki pants, and four pair of boxer shorts, none of which appeared to have been washed in weeks … but no gun.

Similarly, the closet contained only a single, moth-eaten Navy pea coat. Miller played his flashlight over the interior of the closet, but the beam reflected no sign of a trap door. He passed his hand over the single overhead shelf in the closet, feeling nothing on it.

"Come on!" Hagen said, exasperation rasping his voice. "The 'locked room' murder doesn't happen in real life! It's a myth."

"Well, if the guy shot himself, where's the gun?" Miller asked.

"And if someone else shot him, how did they get out with the door chain in place and the only window locked from the inside?" Hagen shot back.

"All right. Let's let the coroner take the body and we'll tear this place apart," Angi said.

After the man's body was removed and the additional light stand was erected in the room – taxing the power supply of the entire hotel – Angi said, "OK, piece by piece. Check everywhere."

After twenty minutes of fruitless searching, Angi stood in the center of the room looking thoroughly perplexed. "Have we looked at every inch of this room, moved every piece of furniture, looked under everything?"

"Yes, ma'am," Hagen and Miller replied in unison.

As she surveyed the room, Angi's eye drifted to the closet and the single shelf at the top. The shelf appeared to be of little use, since it occupied clearly two-thirds of the depth of the tiny room. "How about up there?"

"I felt up there," Miller said. "Nothing."

"Did you *look* up there?"

"Well, no. It's a little higher than my head, but I could reach almost to the back. There was nothing to stand on to actually look, but I'm cert …"

"Well, I'm not," Angi cut him off. "Jared, give me a boost."

"Bingo!" she said a second later. As Hagen lowered her back to the floor, he could see a small package wrapped in oil-paper and a small box of .22 caliber rounds in her gloved hand.

"It was clear at the back of the shelf, but here it is."

Miller caught Hagen's withering glare.

* * *

A week later, Hagen plopped into the gray metal chair next to Angi's desk. "Any news on the DB from last week?"

"Yeah, Jared. The autopsy showed that Low was in the final stages of liver cancer and probably would have lived only a few more days. The ME said that the cause of death, however, was a single .22 caliber bullet to the chest, as we all suspected.

"A .22 didn't have enough power to pass through the body, but was lodged in his heart. Also the chest muscles closed around the wound, accounting for the tiny amount of blood. He bled out internally."

"And all the bullets were accounted for?"

"Yep. And a trace of the serial number of the revolver showed that Low had purchased the gun ten days earlier at the hardware store below the Cali-Ho. The hardware store records showed he also purchased one box of .22 caliber rounds.

"I think that he was despondent over the cancer ripping up his body but still able to pull together the physical stamina he got from years at sea. He lifted his shirt and fired a single shot into his heart."

"But he didn't die immediately?"

"No, it took a while for him to bleed out from the small hole and he was still mobile. Then his sailor's life-long habit of neatly stowing things took over. He replaced the gun in the oil-paper it came in and placed both the gun and the box of bullets on the back of the closet shelf. He left no suicide note because he had no one to leave one for. He then lay down on his last bed … and died on his own schedule. Sad, but it happens."

"Well, there's one other thing, Angi. I got a call this morning from Cavendish, the prop in that place. He was cleaning — and I use the term loosely — Low's room and he found this in a pocket of the coat that was in the closet. I guess we missed it because we were looking for a gun at the time and didn't search the coat for anything else. It's a phone number. The prop thought it might help us locate a next of kin or something."

"Well, we're pretty sure he had no one, but what's the number?"

"I ran a check on it. The number has been disconnected, but the phone company says the number was last installed in a house in San Luis Obispo." There was a glint in Hagen's eye.

"Jared? Let me see that." Angi snatched the small yellowed paper from Hagen's hand.

Written above the phone number was one word — *Teach.*

Chapter 33

11:05 a.m. — August 21. "This is more like it," Teach said as he blew cigarette smoke out the open window of the Cougar. "You said *south* and here we are."

"Yeah, but no more abandoned houses! Remember that," Etta said. "And keep your nasty smoke on your side of the car or put that thing out. I'm not dying of lung cancer because of your filthy habit."

"Yeah, I know," Teach said as he flipped the smoldering butt out the window. "That was too close — again."

The pair had hung around Carson City long enough to read the newspaper account of the rescue of an unnamed teen-aged runaway from an abandoned house in the Washoe Valley. The news story described how authorities were notified by an area resident who saw lights in the supposedly deserted structure. Thankfully, from Place and Teach's perspective, the young victim could only describe their car as 'big and black.'

The detective had withheld from the media the information about finding Teach's fingerprints in the house, or that Etta and her car had been identified. Thus, the criminal pair could not know of the manhunt swirling around them.

But Lady Luck was on their side. They had taken a side trip to Las Vegas, just to lay low for a while, but both were ready to get to their attacks on young girls. They managed to get back into California, and now San Bernardino, without detection.

"You got a new ID?" Etta asked as she pulled to the curb on a downtown street.

"Yeah. Right here," Teach said, waiving the California driver's license knock-off for 'Harvey A. Logan.'

"OK. Get a place rented. I'll meet you back here tomorrow night, 7:00 o'clock. And this time, *be here*, jerkoff."

"Yes, ma'am," Teach said with a mock salute as he slammed the car door.

Etta pulled away and disappeared in the late-morning traffic. Teach never knew where she stayed, nor how to reach her. The nagging feeling that he was the one taking all the chances in this 'partnership' hit him again as he looked around for a phone booth.

* * *

The next evening, the black Mercury glided to the curb in exactly the same spot it had left the day before. A bearded man quickly moved from a nearby doorway and climbed into the passenger seat. The car pulled away from the curb before he even got the door closed.

"What did you get?" Etta asked. As she drove, she scanned the traffic for police cars. She hoped that the cops didn't have a description of her car, but she couldn't be sure. She was still formulating a plan of what to do if she was stopped, especially with Teach in the car.

"I found a rental, just like we got before. It's in a little suburb called Toledo and it's just what we need. I had to give the guy a fake check because he wouldn't take cash. But I had one on a bank in Iowa so it will take a while for him to find out it's bogus. And I found something else!"

"Your brain?" Etta deadpanned.

Teach pretended to ignore her. "When I walked into the rental place, the guy was on the phone bitching to someone about his daughter being out parked in a car with some guy. Apparently there's some kind of scenic overlook on a place called 'Rim of the World Drive' that's not too far from the house. Kids sometimes go up there to park and look out on the city. Sounds like a perfect place to grab our next friend."

"A lover's park? Are you serious? Think about this, dumbass. Yeah, there's young girls there and every one of them is with a young boy. A boy who might report that the girl was grabbed. Or a guy who might play hero and come to some girl's rescue. My mistake. You certainly *did not* find your brain."

Teach gave Etta an exaggerated hurt look.

"Besides, you think that rental guy wouldn't remember you asking about someplace where young girls park? And tell the cops the minute one was reported missing?"

"No. No, Etta. I never asked him about it at all. I got all that stuff from listening to him on the phone. I never let on that I was interested."

"We'll stick to concerts. That's worked the best for us."

* * *

Two nights later, shortly before 11:00 p.m., the Cougar pulled into the turnout that Teach had heard about. There was only one other car in the lot and it was parked a distance away from the overlook area.

"Oh, yeah, this looks promising," Etta spat. "I cannot believe that in an area this big, there isn't one single concert going on this weekend. So we're stuck with this bullshit idea."

"Come on, Etta. Give it a chance. Maybe something will break loose for us."

Twenty minutes later, there were still only two cars in the lot, but there was a definite sign of change in the other car. The windows had been steamed when the kidnappers arrived, but now they could hear angry voices coming from the direction of the car, a mere 30 feet behind them. Teach turned his head and saw a girl, probably about 15, he thought — just the right age — emerge from the right side of the car and slam the door.

"I didn't come up here to have you manhandle me, Greg!" The girl's voice was clear in the cool still air of the late summer night.

"I wasn't ... Come on, Patty. Where are you going?"

"Just leave me alone!"

"OK. OK, cool off. I'll go take a walk so you can calm down. Then I'll take you home. No touching. I promise." The boy started walking away toward the highway.

Ten minutes later, the black car pulled out of the turnout, passing the boy as he was walking back to his car. Patty was nowhere to be seen.

Chapter 34

11:55 p.m. — August 24. It was nearly midnight when the phone rang in the San Bernardino County dispatch center. The young male caller identified himself and told the dispatcher that he thought his girlfriend had been kidnapped. He explained the fight they had and how he had returned to find her missing.

He had driven to the nearest gas station and called her house, but her parents had not heard from her. He had promised to call the police and then return to the girl's home.

"You said there was another car in the lot. Can you describe it?" the dispatcher asked.

"Yeah. I didn't pay much attention at first, but then when I was walking back to see if Patty had cooled down, the car passed me. I noticed that an older woman, maybe 40 or 50 years old, was driving, which seemed strange to me. I mean, usually, it's just kids up there, you know. I did see that she had red hair but that was about all. There was a guy in the car too, but I didn't get a good look at him, other than he had a bushy beard."

"Can you describe the car?" the dispatcher asked again.

"Oh, yeah, sorry. It was a dark colored Mercury. Black, I think, but it could have been dark blue. It had the Mercury logo on the trunk, but I don't know what model it was. I did get the license number though."

"You did? That's great."

"Yeah. It just kind of jumped out at me, because it was my three initials and 610. My birthday is June 10th."

"Great job, Greg. Go to Patty's house and there will be a deputy or a police officer there to meet you and get a full statement from you and the parents."

* * *

Shortly before 1:15 a.m., Etta and Teach returned to the neighborhood where they had prepared the rental house to receive their current victim. The teen-aged girl, Patty, was in the trunk of the Mercury, her hands and feet bound with duct tape. She was gagged with a piece of the venerable adhesive tape. Teach had threatened to kill her if she made noise.

Two blocks from the house, Etta abruptly turned onto a cross street. The turn startled the dozing Teach. "Cops. Roadblock," Etta hissed.

"Were they at the house?"

"No. Looks like they were in the next block or more down, but I didn't get a real good look. We'll just drive around for a while and see if they go away. We've put too much time into this and it's been too long since the last good one for us to panic now."

Two blocks from the rental house and around a corner, a SWAT team surrounded a well-kept house.

"Confirmed, Captain," the SWAT leader radioed the tactical commander. "Black Mercury Montego in the driveway. California license plate matches the description given by the victim's boyfriend. Also, the driver's license description of the woman at this address says she has red hair. The guy's DL photo doesn't show a beard, but he could have grown it since he got the license. He does have dark hair."

"OK, Team One," the commander broadcast. "You're clear for breach."

"On my command," the team leader radioed.

On the leader's command of "Go!," SWAT members with battering rams simultaneously broke down the front and back doors of the small residence. At the sound of the rams hitting the doors, other team members launched tear gas grenades through side windows into the house.

"Chuck, what's happening?" a woman's voice screamed inside the house.

"I don't know! Who are you? Who are you?"

"Police! Get on the floor. Get on the floor, now!"

In less than a minute, the couple lay prone on the floor of their bedroom, their hands bound behind their backs with flexible handcuffs.

"OK, where is she? This will go easier for you if you tell us where the girl is!"

"What girl? What are you talking about?" Chuck asked.

"Man and a woman in your car were up on Rim of the World last night. And now a young girl is missing from there. Don't bullshit us. A witness got your license number and this lady here matches the description of the woman driving the car. Now where is she?"

"Honest, officer. I don't know what you're talking about. My wife and I were home all evening and our car was in the driveway, right where it is now."

"OK, Randy," the commander said as he entered the house. "Let's get them up and see what's going on here."

The SWAT leader nodded to two officers, who pulled the couple to their feet and escorted them, their hands still bound, to chairs in the kitchen.

"The house is clear, Sarge," a SWAT officer said. "No girl here."

"See, I told you," Chuck said. "We weren't up there and we didn't take any girl. We were home all evening."

"Maybe someone took your car without you knowing it?" the SWAT leader asked. Of course, the likelihood of someone stealing a car and then returning it to the owner's driveway was about as remote as the sergeant getting a million dollar pay raise, but the question gave the owner an 'out.' Besides, the man didn't have a beard and it seemed strange that he would have shaved it only an hour or two after the abduction. His story had a ring of truth.

"No, I don't think so. I went out about 9:30 to get something out of the car and it was just where I parked it. Please untie us. We didn't have anything to do with this."

Just then, another SWAT officer entered the room. "I may have an explanation, Sarge. Their car is missing the front license plate."

* * *

"Where are we?" Teach asked groggily as he tried to straighten his body from his awkward sleeping position in the front seat of the Mercury.

"Huh?" Etta mumbled, not yet awake herself. The eastern sky was ablaze with the rising sun and the expanding light revealed the lone car sitting in an open parking lot.

"Oh, yeah," she finally said. "We're in a park somewhere. Remember we pulled in here last night to wait out the cops."

"Um, yeah," Teach said unconvincingly.

"Shit! Do I have to remember everything? You said you were looking for a place for us to hole up too, when I pulled in here. Were you already asleep?"

"I guess ..."

"Never mind. Let's get back to the house before our princess in the trunk starts making a racket. The cops should be gone by now."

Etta didn't mention that she had a good idea why the police were down the street from the rental. She had gone out the evening before and stolen the front license plate from a dark colored car parked in a driveway. *I shouldn't have ripped a plate so close to the rental house but it's too late to worry about that now.* She would never admit to Teach that she made a mistake.

There was a chance that some cop might notice that the Mercury now had only the single plate on the back, but Etta was more concerned that the cops might have traced her own license number. Better to have a cop, and any inadvertent witnesses, see a plate that belonged to another car. Tonight, after the girl was chained up in the rental house, she would take Teach out somewhere further away and have him steal a complete set of license plates for the car.

That plan evaporated when she turned the corner toward the rental house. A city police car was parked at the curb and two cops were standing at the front door of the rental.

"You dumbshit!"

"What did I do now?" Teach protested.

"Cops at the house! Guess it didn't take them so long after all to find out that cashier's check was bogus."

"Now what do we do?"

Etta didn't answer but turned into a driveway and reversed their direction. A short time later, she drove behind a strip mall in nearby San Bernardino. The area, littered with debris from shipping cartons being opened and choked with the stench from long-uncleaned dumpsters, appeared deserted.

"Dump her out!" Etta said as she sat behind the wheel.

A few seconds later, the Mercury re-entered the roadway and moved into traffic on I-15 headed north out of the city.

Ten minutes later, a grocery store employee stepped out the back door of his business to have a smoke and tripped over something lying just outside the door. He picked himself up and stared wide-eyed at the obstruction. It was a girl, bruised, hungry, bound and gagged with duct tape, but alive.

Chapter 35

10:17 a.m. — August 25. Angi was not on-call to respond to any violent crimes that might occur that weekend. She planned to enjoy the beautiful sunny day that was forecast. At least as much as she could.

That morning, she slept late, until 7:20, and leisurely showered. Her only plan for the day was to visit her mother later. It was a sad time of year for Angi, and she welcomed the relaxing quiet. Tchaikovsky's *Piano Concerto #1 in B Flat Minor* playing softly on the cassette deck in the living room.

Today, she was foregoing her usual morning run as she went about preparing her favorite breakfast. The main dish was a soft bagel slathered with a mixture of cream cheese, fresh chervil, salt, and lemon zest. It was then topped with thin slices of smoked salmon, salty capers, and ultra-thin slices of red onion. A glass of her favorite wine, V. Sattui's *Gamay Rouge*, accompanied the bagel.

Angi had first discovered the bagel concoction at a small shop in an out-of-the-way strip mall on the northeast side of the city. Now her own version was a staple of her morning meals whenever she had time to enjoy it. The wine wasn't her usual morning drink, but today would be stressful.

She had just sat down at the small bistro table on her wooden deck outside the back door when the phone rang. *Shit*, she thought, *only two bites of bagel and now a call to screw up my time with Mom.* She took a quick sip of wine before hurrying inside to answer the phone. Even though she was not the designated on-call detective for the weekend, she was still subject to call-out if a major crime requiring multiple investigators occurred.

"Angi, it's Roger," the voice on the phone said.

"Roger! I haven't heard from you in a while." The call was a surprise to her. She and her ex-husband had been friends since they were teenagers and had casually dated in high school. After Angi returned from college and joined the police department, the two were reunited by Angi's closest high school friend. They began dating and, within a few months, were married.

The union was short-lived. Roger, although an intelligent, happy and friendly man, was inwardly reserved. His job as manager of a large shoe store in the mall fit his personality perfectly. But his nature was in sharp contrast to the decisiveness and boldness of his new bride. And it seemed to him that his wife was more wedded to her job than to him. The feeling, growing more evident the longer they lived together, soon began to overwhelm him.

Eight months after they were married, Roger and Angi divorced. It was an amicable parting and they remained friends, although they didn't talk often.

"Yeah. I know I missed your birthday, but I've been thinking about you lately. About you and your mom." Even when their union was dissolving, Angi's mother had been kind to Roger.

"Thanks, Roger. I appreciate that." Angi wasn't sure what else to say. The whole thing had soured her on the idea of marriage. *You can't be good at a job like mine and still have time for a husband,* she rationalized. Still, she enjoyed seeing Roger from time to time, if only because she could count on him not to ask about whatever case she was working on.

"I was thinking. I know you try to visit your mom every Sunday if you're not working."

Angi nodded silently as she held the phone. Her mother. The woman who had to endure some of the worst that life could throw at a woman. Rose Masters had always seemed to be such a strong presence in their house. That was until that terrible August afternoon in 1956, a clear and sunny day just like today.

Angi, then almost eight years old, and her friend, Nancy, were playing in Angi's room, whiling away the time before school started again. They had been outside in the backyard, wistfully gazing at the cool water in the pool, before Rose called them back inside. She would not permit the girls to be in the pool without her supervision.

Waiting for Rose to give them permission to play in the backyard swimming pool, they had to be content with Angi's dolls for the moment. Suddenly, they heard a horrific scream. They ran downstairs to find Rose pulling the lifeless body of Angi's four-year-old sister, Karen, from the pool.

Outwardly, Rose placed the blame for the loss of her second child on her husband, Don. The latch on the sliding glass door leading to the pool had been broken for months, but he had put off fixing it. Don Masters readily took the blame on himself. The couple could not move past the tragedy and a year later, they separated.

Don moved to an apartment across town and still saw Angi on weekends, but it was never the same. At first, Don seemed to try to compensate by buying Angi anything she wanted. Sometimes be bought things she hadn't even thought about, but nothing eased his guilt. Gradually, his depression increased and, when Angi was 13, she came home from school to learn that her father had killed himself by crashing his car into a tree at high speed.

Rose had focused the blame for Karen's death on the faulty latch, as much to suppress her own guilt as any blame she truly placed on her husband. Karen had been playing in the room next to the kitchen where Rose was working, but the toddler had managed to get outside without her mother's notice. Her own demons eventually took her to an extended care psychiatric facility.

Even Angela herself was haunted by the tragedy. She mourned the breakup of her parents' marriage and the loss of her father. But she was most personally affected by her sister's death.

Karen had gotten outside through the only door leading to the pool. But she was not strong enough to open the heavy door — unless it was left open a crack so that she could get her little hands on the edge of the door to slide it back. Did Angi close the door completely when she and Nancy came in from the back yard that day? She would never know, but that day and its aftermath would regularly invade her psyche.

"If it's ok with you, I'd like to go along. I haven't seen her in a long time and I still think the world of her," Roger said, breaking the silence on the line.

"I'm sure she would love to see you, Roger, but maybe another time. I missed seeing her last weekend and it was the anniversary of ... well, you know. Anyway, I'd like this weekend to just to be for the two of us. You understand, don't you?"

"Of course, Angi. I should have thought of that. What's it been? Twenty-nine years?"

"Yeah. She would have been 33 now."

"Your mom needs you to be with her. I'll give you a call in a couple of weeks and maybe we can go together then."

An hour later, Angi parked her green Saab in the parking lot of the care center. She sat in the car for several minutes, staring vacantly out the window. *This anniversary visit gets tougher every year.*

Angi walked into the private room holding a bouquet of lilies and roses, her mother's two favorite flowers.

"Hi, Mama."

The older woman's face lit up. "Karen? Karen, is that you?"

Chapter 36

9:10 a.m. — August 26. "Detective Masters, this is Detective Mark Morgan in San Luis Obispo," the voice on the phone said.

"Were you able to find the house?"

"Yes, we did. The phone number you got led us right to it, after a little delay in getting a warrant to get the phone company to release the location."

"Does it look like your victim was held there?"

"Yeah. The basement of the house was pretty much like you described in the other scenes. Mattress on the floor and signs that someone was chained to the wall. Our crime scene techs are still there, looking for anything that would put Teach or our victim in the house."

"What about the rental company?"

"This one was rented directly by the owner, or more correctly, the owner's representative. The owner is a prominent lawyer who owns three or four of these run-down houses. I doubt he's ever seen any of them himself, but he has some clerk in his office who handles the rentals. In this case, they took cash and didn't get much information. What they did get was phony, ID and prior address and such. However, the clerk picked Teach out of a photo array as the guy who rented it."

"Blood in the place?"

"Not really. I mean, what I saw was a little blood on the mattress and a little on a support post. I forgot to mention that it looks like our victim was tied to a post and beaten, just like you described the others. But no sign that she was hacked up like Detective Anderson described your victim.

"I'm going back out to check on the neighbor interviews, but I haven't heard of anyone seeing anything suspicious so f ... Hold on a second."

After a few seconds, the detective came back on the line. "Let me call you back, Detective. I was just told that our crime scene people may have found our victim."

Ten minutes later, Morgan called Angi's direct phone line again. "We found her. The techs found her body in an old freezer in a back corner of the basement. They can't tell me a lot yet, because the body has been there so long, but apparently the freezer seals kept the decomp gases from getting out to alert the neighbors. Most likely, the owner's people never came around."

"Was she ...?

"Can't tell, of course, if she was raped, although the tech said she was nude in the freezer. But her body is intact."

* * *

"OK, Devon. Help me out with this," Angi said as she sat down in Anderson's guest chair. The chair was the same gray metal military surplus chair as the one next to Angi's desk. The thin sheet of foam under the cheap Naugahyde cover of the seat wasn't designed for the occupant's comfort. But then, detectives rarely sat down next to each other's desks.

"With what, Ang?"

"The Fire Storm murder." Devon himself had given that nickname to the case of the brutally murdered and dismembered young woman. The case happened during a real fire storm above Fountaingrove. And the fire storm of protest from the residents still seemed to lurk just beneath the surface, despite Angi's efforts to assure them. They wanted answers about what had happened in their neighborhood. They wanted to feel safe. And Angi, the lead investigator, could give them neither.

"You mean why was our victim the only one dismembered? At least that we know of," he said.

"Exactly. I've been mulling this thing all weekend — well, except for a little time out to see my mom — and I can't get a handle on it."

"I can maybe see cutting off the hand when she was running around the neighborhood screaming for help and putting her hands on people's houses. Just maybe. Hell, maybe it was an accident. The guy lashed out at her with a knife or something and it was an accident. But why do the rest of it?"

"And why throw the head on the roof of the house next door?" Devon said. "That's the part that bugs me and I'm pretty hardened, if I do say so myself. That is really sicko."

"Yeah, it is. And to me, it doesn't fit either." Angi gazed at the wall, her mind sorting her thoughts. "The other body parts were put into a plastic bag, not thrown around. We still don't know what happened to the other hand, but that would be a pretty definite trail to ID'ing the victim. So it makes some sense that he would dispose of it."

"Maybe he didn't remember where the other hand, the one Kim found, was exactly. Or he was too spooked to go out and look for it."

"Tell me this, Devon. Do you think the woman was a part of this? I mean, more than luring the girls to a place where Teach could subdue them?"

"Yeah. At least to some degree. Remember the girl in Nevada said that the woman — what's her name? Place? — raped her too. And the woman was the one who beat her when she was tied to the pole. But butchering up the body? That strikes me more as a male thing."

"But to me, the clean up, putting the body parts in a plastic bag and tying it up, and then carrying it out to the lake to dispose of it — that sounds more like a woman. Why not just leave the body in the house like they did in SLO?"

"Sorry, Angi. I don't have any answers to this one. But there's only one question that matters right now. Where are they now and can we get them before they kill again?"

Chapter 37

2:14 p.m. — August 26. It didn't take long for Angi to get the answer to at least part of her dilemma.

"Detective Masters, this is Detective Abe Ramirez in San Bernardino. I think we just missed your Bonnie and Clyde."

"Well, I certainly wouldn't call them that, Detective, but what do you have?"

Ramirez outlined finding the kidnapping victim, Patty, behind the grocery store. "She is bruised, mostly from being banged around in the trunk of a car. Otherwise, she couldn't tell us much because from the time she was taken until she was dumped behind the store, she was never out of the trunk."

"Did she see the kidnappers?"

"Yeah, a little. She said she was walking around, crying, in a parking lot at a scenic outlook after a fight with her boyfriend. She noticed another car parked in the lot but just thought it was probably another teen-aged couple. She didn't approach the car because she didn't want to be embarrassed if it was someone she and her boyfriend knew.

"Anyway, she said a red-haired woman, probably in her 40's, got out of the other car in the parking lot and approached her, asking if she was ok. The woman seemed kind, so she was telling her what happened. Then a man grabbed her from behind.

She started to scream, but the man put his hand over the girl's mouth and the woman told her they would kill her if she made a sound. Then the man, who she described and short, maybe 5'8 or 5'9 with a wild curly black beard, taped her wrists with duct tape.

They made her walk to their car and the woman told her to get in the trunk. She shook her head 'no' because she was afraid, but the man got right up in her face and threatened again to kill her if she didn't comply. After she got in the trunk, he bound her ankles and put a piece of tape over her mouth. She was left there until she was dumped in the alley the next day."

"Well, that sounds like our suspects, Teach and Place. But without at least a tentative ID, how did you wind up calling me?"

"Strangest thing. The boyfriend got a license number from the other car as it was leaving the parking lot. That was before he knew the girl was missing because he had gone for a walk after the fight. Anyway, he happened to remember the license number because it was his initials and birth date. Weird, huh."

"OK. Go on."

"So it came back to a car registered in one of the small suburban towns in the county. The local PD found the car in the driveway and the general description of the car and the license number matched, so their SWAT team hit the house. But after they got the couple inside contained, they determined that they weren't the suspects. Then they discovered that the front license plate of the couple's car had been stolen."

"Shit. That sucks."

"Yeah, but it sounds like the chief out there, a pretty good guy, got it smoothed over, although the city is facing a big bill to fix up their house. Anyway, it was all up in the air until some guy at a rental company called in to report that he had rented a house to a real sleazy looking guy and that the guy had paid with a forged cashier's check."

"OK, now this is starting to make sense. Did you find them at the house?" *You better hope your answer is no. I'll come down there and strangle you myself if you have them in custody and you've buried that information in 15 minutes of background.*

"Unfortunately, no. However, the rental is only a couple of blocks from the house where the license plate was stolen. So the PD put two and two together and called us to see if we had any information. I was talking to them when the call came in about the girl being found in our city. Our crime scene people helped them process the house and found some prints belonging to Edward Teach. Also, the rental guy ID'd him from his mug shot as the renter. The state had a flag on the prints with a message to call you, and here we are.

"And the techs also found a mattress and a chain setup just like you described in your flyer. So it looks like your perps have moved south."

"No ID of the woman, though?"

"No. We were hoping that you could give us something on that."

"The woman who has been with Teach, and the only one as far as we know, is named Henrietta Place. She has a couple of prostitution arrests but that's about all I've found on her. I can FAX you her package. Also, she drives a '79 black Mercury Cougar. The plate number will be in the package too."

"Well, that makes quite a bit of sense. She's probably running with a different plate now, because the stolen plate I was telling you about — the one from a couple of blocks from the rental. It was taken from a 1980 black Mercury Montego. We've put out an all-points-bulletin on that plate but I'm guessing they'll anticipate that and cop another plate somewhere."

"But your victim is safe, unharmed?"

"Yes, thank God. From the description in your flyer, it sounds like she was incredibly lucky to get away with just some bruises from the trunk."

"And she wasn't a runaway?"

"No. No. Not at all?"

"Shit. They're changing their MO. This will make it even harder to collar them." Angi's mind reeled with the possibilities.

"One thing. The girl said the car was very still for a long time. She thinks they were parked somewhere, maybe sleeping. She also drifted off to sleep, but then woke up when the car started moving. She said they were just driving along, when all of a sudden, she heard the woman swear really loud and the car made a sharp turn. She thinks they pulled into a driveway, because of the way they only went a short distance after the turn, and then backed up and seemed to go the other way. A short time later, she was dumped out."

"So you're thinking they were maybe headed back to the house to start raping the victim as they have in the past, but saw the police car out front, investigating the bad check?"

"That's exactly how I read it. Plus, the chief in Toledo told me that they had a couple of blocks in each direction cordoned off for the SWAT operation, and the rental was inside that perimeter."

"So they couldn't get back to their terror house immediately after they snatched the girl, as they've done in the past. Sounds like they're getting sloppy, or just unlucky. But either way, let's hope that works in our favor, and definitely in the favor of potential victims."

"Well, they're in the wind now. Let us know what we can do to help. We'll follow up on any lead or tactic you think might help."

"As soon as I think of one, Detective, I'll let you know."

Chapter 38

8:40 a.m. — August 27. "So do you have a plan, Angi?" Sergeant Garrison asked.

"Yes, but you'll think I'm crazy, Boss."

Garrison just smiled at his favorite detective. He had trained her as a rookie and had also requested her for assignment to violent crimes when others didn't think she was ready for 'the big time.'

"She needs to spend a little more time in burglary," the lieutenant had said. Garrison didn't expect that 'Clouseau' would support his request, but he knew that, ultimately, the chief would. Lieutenant Clews knew that, too.

"She's making more arrests than the rest of the property squad put together, and Sergeant Krohn supports my request to transfer her." The property crimes supervisor had nodded his agreement.

"Fine! You'll have to live with this decision, Garrison." Lieutenant Clews had scribbled his approval on the transfer form, threw it at Garrison like a petulant child, then turned his back on the sergeants. They shot knowing glances at each other and left the office without a word.

Angi sometimes came up with some unorthodox strategies. Garrison had also heard about some things she supposedly had done, but he decided he would rather not know the details. Still, she solved cases and those cases stuck in court.

"Oh, something crazy, huh. Well, there's a first time for everything, Detective Masters. Let's hear it."

"Well, we know that they like to rent houses in middle income areas to hold their victims. They've done that in every case we know about, except in Nevada. Well, we don't know for sure about Merced, but it's probably a safe bet that they didn't leave blood around. The owner might just have cleaned the place without realizing there had been someone held captive there."

"OK."

"So I think we should notify every property rental agency in the state, the ones that deal in residential property at least. We know the MO is to pay initially with cash. Then if they need to pay additional rent, they do it with a phony cashier's check. We have photos of both Teach and Place which witnesses tell us are pretty good likenesses, so we distribute those in the flyers to the rental places."

"Well, it's not a crazy idea," Garrison smiled. "It's a logistical nightmare, but not crazy."

"Yeah, but we don't have to do it ourselves. We put together a sample flyer that we send to every law enforcement agency in the state. We already have them in our database. Then we ask them to make contact with every rental agency in their jurisdiction. *And*, we leave a place on the flyer for each agency to put their own contact name and phone number. That way, they are screening for us and they get the credit if something turns up in their jurisdiction. Win - win all the way."

"Devon, Julie, do you have any thoughts on this?"

"I think it might work," Phelps said. "Sure it will take some work for our clerks. But our BOLO inquiries to other departments haven't turned up anything in two months, except after a kidnapping happened. Maybe this will let some department be the hero by getting in ahead of the crime."

"I agree with Angi and Julie," Anderson said. "This boils down to old-fashioned leg work and you know I believe in that. Besides, it fits in with that new community policing thing that the chief is pushing. Except that in this case, the community is the whole state."

"I agree. Go ahead, Angi. Talk to records and see if they can cut a clerk or two loose to work with our secretaries to put the whole thing together under your direction."

Angi nodded. *I hope to hell this works.*

* * *

"Doesn't this I-15 take us back towards Las Vegas?" Teach asked.

"Wow. The sailor can read a map." Etta's contempt for her partner seemed to leach into her comments more often lately, after two narrow escapes. "Yeah, that's what I want the cops to believe, just in case anybody saw us and got a license plate number."

At Cajon Junction, the Mercury left the interstate and headed northwest on highway 138. An hour later, the two kidnappers ambled into a roadside diner in Lancaster. After wolfing down a couple of hamburgers with all the trimmings, they again headed north. But this time, the Mercury carried Kansas license plates, unwittingly supplied by a tourist family who were also eating in the diner.

Etta didn't stop until she had cut across several other secondary roads to wind up on Interstate 5. It was nearly 10:00 p.m. when she pulled into a seedy motel on the outskirts of Lost Hills. She had a destination in mind, but was not sharing it with Teach, at least not yet.

The next morning, the pair was on the road by 7:00 a.m. "I don't want to be in one place too long, at least until we can get another set of plates, preferably ones that won't be reported stolen for a while," Etta said.

"Etta, I used to live in Merced County," Teach said. "There's an old car salvage place not too far off the interstate near Los

Banos. Maybe we can sneak in there and cop a set of plates from a car that's going to be crushed. No one will notice that."

"Sounds like a good idea, for a change. How far away is it?"

Teach smiled. "No more than a couple of hours, I'd guess."

"Good idea, *except* that we would be getting there at 9:30 on a Wednesday morning. So what are you thinking? We should just walk into the office and say, 'hey, we're here to steal some license plates. Do you mind?' "

"OK, so we might have to hole up for a little while. We could get some breakfast or something. I'm starved anyway."

"Yeah. Walking into the office at noon *would* be a better plan. Oh, yeah, I forgot. *Thinking* isn't your strong point."

"Etta, why are you always busting my balls? I put up with your bullshit a lot, but I used to be in charge of a lot of people. I know how to figure things out."

"You were a petty officer third class, and had that rank for only three weeks before you were kicked out of the Navy. I've seen your papers, remember. You weren't in charge of your own shit."

"No, you're wrong. I was ..."

"You were *what*? An officer? *Please*. That Navy lieutenant's uniform you were wearing when I met you was one you lifted from somewhere. You were just wearing it because you thought girls were more attracted to all the shiny shit on your collar."

"Worked on you, didn't it?" Teach grinned uncomfortably.

"Yeah, and look where I am now!"

Chapter 39

10:14 a.m. — September 6. Ed Teach roused from a deep sleep in the cheap motel outside Redding. It took him a few minutes to fully realize where he was. It was the fifth place that he and Etta had stayed in the past eight days.

Etta was already awake, sitting in the solitary chair in the room, a thread-bare Chesterfield which sat in the corner next to the window. She stared vacantly at the parking lot, only marginally aware that Teach was awake.

"Hey, Etta. You wanna get some breakfast?"

"Huh? Oh, yeah, Ed. That would be nice."

What's gotten into her? She never calls me 'Ed.'

"This is a helluva life, isn't it?" Etta said, returning her gaze to the parking lot.

"Yeah?" *Where is this going?*

"I coulda been just as good as Angela Masters or Caroline Suydam, you know."

"Who?"

"Nothing. Just a couple of goodie two-shoe girls I used to know. You know, I wasn't even there when my mom died. I was in some rat-hole dive in Nevada. I didn't even know about it for a week."

Teach said nothing. *I've never seen her down like this. Yeah, we've had some bad luck on the last couple of grabs, but shit! She's always been the badass.*

"Alright," Etta said, wiping a tear from her cheek. "Let's get the hell out of here and get some fucking breakfast."

* * *

It was nearly noon when Etta and Teach returned to the motel room. "Did you believe that bitch?" Etta's mood was almost light-hearted. " 'We don't serve breakfast after 10:30,' " she said, mocking the waitress at the first restaurant they had visited. "I wanted to say, 'What the fuck, bitch. Your grill only work for eggs 'til 10:30 and then it spits them on the floor?' Better yet, I shoulda pulled my little blade and carved my initials in her fucking cheek."

"Come on, Etta. We got a good meal. That second place served all day breakfast, and it tasted great to me."

"Yeah, it was nice to make like normal people, even if it's just for a little while."

"Yeah, I'm feeling good and I could use me a girl. Any concerts going on in this town?"

"Damn, Teach! You couldn't let me have one good moment?"

Shit! So much for her good mood. "I'm sorry, Etta. Never mind. We can talk about it later."

"No, no, Eddie."

Eddie?!

"Come on. You want a good fuck. I'll give you one," Etta said coyly as she pulled her top over her head.

Etta and Ed had phenomenal sex when they first met. But since the first kidnapping, there had been no intimate contact between her and Teach, although she had been suggestive on occasion.

"Come on, honey," she said as she lay on the rumpled bed in her underwear. "Come to mama. Then afterward, if you want, we can find you a pretty young thing."

Teach warily eyed the nightstand and bed for any signs of the hobby knife. *What is with this change in her mood?* Teach's concerns with the radical change in Etta's demeanor left him unfulfilled. Still, he hoped Etta believed him when he told her the sex was great.

"Nothing is too good for my Eddie. Soon, we can get you another honey. But I need to make a stop first." She returned to the Chesterfield and again gazed absent-mindedly out the window.

* * *

"I think I figured it out, Jules," Angi said four days later.

"Figured what out, Angi? Have I mentioned that sometimes you start a conversation in the middle of a thought?"

Angi winked, but didn't acknowledge Phelps' comment. "How Low and Teach are connected. They knew each other from the Navy. And both of them were given dishonorable discharges at about the same time."

"So you think Low was involved in the kidnappings and murders?"

"No, he seems to be more of a behind-the-scenes kind of guy. But get this. After the Navy, Low got a job with a printer in Los Angeles."

"So you're thinking that Low supplied the phony IDs that Teach used to rent the house here and in SLO?"

"Doesn't that make sense? Low had the phone number for the house in San Luis Obispo. He probably had to call Teach to set up the exchange. Maybe he made multiple IDs."

"Pretty good forgeries, though, for a guy who just worked in some print shop."

"He had what, fifteen years or so to perfect his craft."

"And then gets cancer and winds up killing himself in one of the worst flop houses we have in this city."

"I'm rethinking that too. We'll never know, of course, but maybe he read about what happened to Abby and somehow made the connection to Teach. What if he offed himself, not because of the cancer, but because he couldn't handle being connected to Teach's off-the-wall crimes?"

"You'll have to ask Teach about that when we catch him." Phelps' voice showed no doubt that Teach would be caught.

"Oh, I will, Jules. Believe me, I have lots of questions for Mr. Teach."

* * *

"Angi, I'm glad to see you're back," Devon said as he walked into the conversation.

"What's up?"

"We just got another report of a teen-aged girl being kidnapped. It looks like it might be Teach's work."

"Where?"

"Portland, Oregon. They called about 20 minutes ago. They had a 14-year-old runaway who was last seen at a concert in Portland last Friday night. The surveillance video from the venue shows her walking away with a bearded man."

"Damn! San Bernardino and now Portland. These creeps are all over the place, and who knows what else they've done in the past month. Did you tell them about the rental angle?"

"Yes. They're checking on that, but Portland is a good-sized city. It will probably take a while."

"Yeah. A while that this girl doesn't have."

"I also gave them a description of Place's Mercury. It seems that she won't abandon that car, but we know that she's stolen plates for it before so that's not going to help them a whole lot."

"And all we can do is wait — and pray."

Chapter 40

6:15 a.m. — September 15. Angi was up early. She had brought the case summary file for the so-called Fire Storm case home to pore over it. There had to be something she missed, some bit of information that would lead her to the brutal killers.

The frustration at having no idea where they had gone since they left San Bernardino nearly a month before only increased her concern that another girl's life was in danger. And if they were, in fact, the ones who had taken the girl in Portland, Angi knew she had to find an answer fast.

Roger would be there at 10:00. He had called her the preceding Friday and they had agreed that he could go with her to visit her mother that Sunday. That gave her a few hours to go over the case file and enjoy a quiet breakfast before visiting her mother. She had also agreed to have an early dinner with her ex-husband, so this was her only chance today to find the elusive clue, if there was anything there.

She had started her third pass through the file, reading every summary report created by any detective or officer involved in the case. But so far, nothing jumped out at her as a new lead. She had lost track of the time and was startled when the doorbell rang.

Closing the file, she answered the door. "Hi, Roger. I'm sorry but I got distracted." She didn't mention that she was reading a case file. That had been a contentious issue during their marriage — her penchant for bringing her work home — and she saw no reason to bring it up.

"Have a seat and I'll get dressed. It will only take a minute."

Ten minutes later, she re-entered the living room to see Roger looking at her open case file.

"Roger, you know you shouldn't be reading that." She tried to make the admonition gentle but was also mentally kicking herself for leaving the file on the coffee table.

"Sorry, Angi. I know. I only looked at the first page or two, but I have one question."

Oh, shit. Now I'm going to have to tell him something that I probably shouldn't or completely dodge his question. Either way, it might screw-up what otherwise should be a good day with an old friend. "What is it, Rog?"

"I'm just wondering why you have a picture of Janice in your file."

"Janice? Janice who?" *There's no 'Janice' connected with this case.*

"Right here in the front, you have her picture. Janice Smith. She was a year ahead of us at Montgomery High."

I thought there was something familiar about her in the picture, but I couldn't place it. "I really don't remember her. Are you sure?"

"Yeah. You probably wouldn't have known her. She was pretty introverted and plain-looking and she didn't participate in many activities. But I got to know her when we were both in Spanish Club. And back then, she was a lot slimmer and her hair was a lot darker, but still red."

"I kind of remember seeing her around, now that you mention it. But she's changed a lot."

"Yeah, I probably wouldn't have picked up on it if I hadn't seen her recently."

"You did? When?"

"She came into the store, oh — let me think — probably three or four months ago. Right before the Fourth of July holiday, I think. At first I didn't recognize her but I could tell she was acting like she knew me. So after a little bit, she came over to the counter and told me who she was. It was good to see her."

"Did she tell you anything about what she's been doing? Where she lives?"

"No, not that I remember. But I do remember one thing that jumped out at me. Her dad is in the same care facility as your mother."

Angi tried to suppress her shock. "Was there anyone with her?"

"Come to think of it, yeah. At least, I think there was a guy with her. I mean, I never saw them actually together, but he came in about the same time and left about the same time. He just looked around at some shoes but didn't ask to try on anything."

"Do you remember what he looked like?"

"Short guy. Maybe 5'8 or so. The main thing was this big bushy black beard and long hair. The guy reminded me of a pirate or something." Roger chuckled at the thought.

Angi pulled another photo from two pages back in the file. "Is this the guy?"

"Sure could be. That's the beard, that's for sure."

"Thanks, Rog. That helps me a lot."

"Can I ask what the case is about. I only saw the cover page and Janice's picture clipped to the front."

Angi cocked her eyebrow. "Can't right now, Roger. But you have no idea how much you've helped."

Forty-five minutes later, Roger's car pulled into the care facility's parking lot with Angi in the passenger seat. It was all Angi could do to concentrate on visiting her mother and not asking the staff about Mr. Smith — and any visitors he might have had.

* * *

The next morning, Angi was at work by 6:30. "Get me anything you can find on a Janice Smith, probably born in '46 or '47, originally from Santa Rosa," Angi said to the records clerk. "Her father's name is Gerald. Also, anything you might have on him or any other family members."

Back at her desk, Angi opened the Montgomery High School yearbook from 1965, the year before she graduated. Fortunately, she had kept all her old yearbooks at home. Flipping to the 'S' section of the senior class, her eyes were immediately drawn to the photo of Janice E. Smith.

The girl had her hair put up in a large beehive, the hairstyle of the day, heavily teased and held in place with copious amounts of sticky hairspray. She wore a plain gray-collared, red satin drape, the senior photo uniform of every female graduate of Montgomery.

Just as Roger had told her, the girl in the picture was far slimmer than the person depicted in the mug shot photo of 'Henrietta Place.' Although the yearbook photo was in black and white, it seemed to Angi that the girl's hair was considerably darker than the almost carrot-red hue of Place's hair. That also matched what Roger had told her.

Looking closely at the faces in the two photos, Angi was certain they were the same person. Still, she might never have made the connection between the fugitive Place and her high school classmate had it not been for Roger's information.

"I'm gonna get you now, Etta, or Janice, or whatever the hell you want to call yourself. I'm gonna get you!"

"What did you say, Angi?" Julie Phelps asked from her desk fifteen feet away.

"Nothing, Jules. Just talking to myself." Angi smiled.

Chapter 41

9:00 a.m. — September 16. Angi parked in a visitor's spot near the front door of the high school. It had been nearly five years since she had been in the building, despite it being her alma mater. She went to the office, still in its familiar location.

"Is Mr. Silas in?"

"I'm sorry, ma'am. Principal Silas retired two years ago. Is there anyone el ...?"

"Angela? Angela Masters?" said a voice from the principal's office.

"Mrs. Montrose? Are you ...?"

"Yes, I'm the principal now. Come in. Come in. How are you?"

"It's great to see you, Mrs. Montrose."

"Please sit down, Angi. And please, call me Doris. We're not in sophomore English class anymore."

"Thank you. I'm actually here on official business."

"Yes. Detective, isn't it? I've followed you in the *Sun*, and a few times on TV. I always knew you would do well, although I have to confess I thought it would be whipping the Russians as part of Team USA Volleyball."

"Times change, Doris. Anyway, I'm here about Janice Smith, class of '65. Do you remember her?"

"Vaguely, but let me get her file." A few minutes later, the principal had finished reviewing the old student file. "Yes, I did have her in my English class. Quiet girl. Average student. I remember the red hair. But I'm afraid there's not much else I can tell you. It doesn't look like we've had any contact with her since she graduated."

"What about family?"

"Says here that her father's name is Gerald and that he was a car salesman. Her mother was a homemaker. I think I remember hearing that she passed away a few years ago. I'd have to research the district records to find out more about that."

"That's ok. I don't need that now. What about siblings?"

"Hmmm ... one brother, Nathan. Graduated from Montgomery in '62. I can check his file for an address."

* * *

Forty five minutes later, Angi knocked on the door frame of a small office in the city Public Works Department. The plaque on the wall next to the door read, 'Nathan G. Smith, Assistant City Engineer.'

"Mr. Smith, I'm Detective Angela Masters. Can we talk privately?"

"I'm afraid I can't tell you much, Detective," the man said when the door was closed. "I haven't heard from my sister in more than ten years."

"Can you tell me what happened?

"Right after high school — this would have been probably 1967 — she married a guy named Ben Allenton. He was from up around Ukiah somewhere. Nice guy but I never knew much about him. They seemed to get along fine and were living in a little place up in Mount Prospect."

"That's on the coast highway up by Eureka, right?"

"Further north than that, but yes. Ben was working as a clerk in a convenience store. They didn't have much money, but seemed happy. Then one day in late 1969, a guy held up the convenience store. Somehow, Ben managed to trip the alarm and the police showed up while the robber was still inside.

"After a while, a guy in a ski mask came out the front door holding a gun to a guy's head. The cops ordered him to drop his gun but he never said anything. I guess after them telling him to drop it several times and him not doing it, a cop got a shot off. Turned out that the robber had made Ben put on the ski mask and act like he was holding the real robber hostage. The gun wasn't loaded and the guy told Ben that he had a friend holding Janice hostage."

"Was Ben ok?"

"No. The cop only shot him in the arm, but the bullet hit the big artery in his upper arm and he bled to death before the ambulance could get there. Nobody had been holding Janice. That was all a lie. She was adamant that the cops deliberately killed her husband. After raising hell for a couple of months and getting nowhere, she just disappeared. I haven't seen or heard from her since like March or April, 1970."

"Has Janice ever been arrested?"

"Not that I know of. Definitely not before 1969, 1970. After that, I don't know."

"Thank you, Mr. Smith."

"Do you know where she is, Detective? Is she all right?"

"No, Mr. Smith, I'm sorry. I don't know where she is. But if she contacts you or any of your family, please call me right away."

* * *

"Nothing in any state or federal record on Janice Smith, or Janice Allenton. Not with the DOB you got from the school," the clerk told Angi when she returned to the violent crimes office. "I ran both names with just a year of birth of 1947, too. Of course, there are a ton of Janice Smiths out there, even with the single birth year. But I couldn't find anything that looks like it matches your suspect. And nothing on any Janice Allenton with a birth date in 1947 at all."

"Can you run Henrietta Lucinda Place, with a DOB, of … that's interesting. Sorry, with a DOB of 12-12-52 in all western states? Actually, check that name with any DOB. It's pretty unique. You already gave me a couple of arrests for her in the City and in Oakland in '80 and '81. But I have a gap of about ten years in her life that I need to account for."

Angi stared in the direction of the departing clerk. *She gave her DOB as 1952 when she was arrested, but Janice Smith was born in 1947. She must have gotten hold of a pretty good forged ID, likely a driver's license, for the arresting officers to put down the 1952 date with certainty. Now, where and when did she get it?*

"Sarah, wait! Could you also run a DL check on that name as far back as you can go in all the western states?"

Chapter 42

10:10 a.m. — September 18. So far, the records inquiries had not turned up any information beyond what Angi already knew. She was mulling her options when her phone rang, a transfer call from the records division.

"Detective Masters, this is Detective Pat Dennison in Elko, Nevada. I saw your teletype requesting information on a Janice E. Allenton."

"Yes, Detective. Thanks for calling. Do you have a record on her?"

"No, no record. She's deceased."

"Really? Janice Eleanor Smith Allenton, DOB 10-14-1947."

"Yes, ma'am. That's her. Well, I didn't know about the 'Smith' part, but Janice E. Allenton was the name on her driver's license."

"Can you tell me what happened?

"It happened in December 1975. Ms. Allenton was working as a prostitute here in Elko — you know that prostitution is legal in Elko County, right?"

"I knew it was legal in most of Nevada, yes."

"Anyway, she was sharing an old house with another prostitute. There was a fire that destroyed the whole house. Her roommate was gone at the time, but came home about the time the fire department was getting the last of the blaze knocked down. She asked about Smith, but no one was aware of anyone being in the house.

"But during the mop-up, the firefighters found a woman's body. The body was too badly burned for any identification, but the roommate said that Smith was the only one who would have been in the house. She was adamant that they never entertained clients in their home."

"What happened to the body?"

"She was buried in the county cemetery here in Elko. We recovered her Nevada driver's license from her purse which was in a cabinet and wasn't burned too badly. But it had the address of the house that burned. The roommate didn't know where she came from — not an unusual circumstance — and we had nothing to go on."

"One more question, Detective. Do you have the roommate's name and info?"

"Yeah, right here. Her name was Place, Henrietta Lucinda Place, DOB 12-12-1952."

"Did the fire department determine an origin and cause?"

"Origin and cause? Do they teach fire terms to homicide detectives there in Santa Rosa?"

"No," Angi chuckled. "But one of my partners was assigned to the arson unit before he came to violent crimes, so I picked up a little of the lingo. Probably just enough to be dangerous."

"OK. Just wondered. We have to be a little more cross-trained here. Smaller agency. Anyway, in answer to your question, the cause was officially ruled as 'undetermined.' The origin was an electric cook top in the kitchen. There was a bunch of paper, mostly mail and old newspapers, piled on the cook top. It apparently got turned on somehow and that's what set the whole thing off.

"We asked the roommate about it. She said that neither one of them could cook very well so they never used the cook top. They just used it as an extra counter space and threw the bills and newspapers on there."

"And no idea how the burner got turned on?"

"No. The knob was charred in the fire, so no chance of prints. We couldn't rule out Place, the roommate, but a clerk at a motel she used for her tricks remembered seeing her there that night. He couldn't be specific as to the time, and of course, we couldn't locate the john she said she was with. It seemed a little hinky to me, but there was nothing we could hold her on."

* * *

"I know how she did it, Mike," Angi said as she walked into Garrison's office.

"How who did what?"

"How Janice Smith Allenton became Henrietta Place." She recounted the information she had just received from the Elko detective.

"So nothing to tie Smith to the fire, but it was really Place that was killed?"

"Exactly. Smith wanted to disappear and it was the perfect situation. The body was burned beyond recognition and even if they got dental impressions, they didn't know where to look for a match. So Smith just adopted Place's identity. With it probably came a legitimate Nevada driver's license. That's how she came to have a valid California DL when she was arrested in the City. She just surrendered a valid Nevada license to get her California one. Nothing to red-flag that at all.

"The San Francisco arrest was probably her first. She had been working as a prostitute in Nevada, where it is legal. I'm guessing she was in the City for some reason and picked up a john to get some quick cash. She probably wasn't even thinking about the law difference, and got popped."

"So what is your next move?"

"Hopefully, she's tried to visit her father recently."

* * *

That afternoon, Angi checked back with the care facility staff. "Thank you for seeing me, Doctor. I'm investigating a homicide, the death of the young woman whose body was recovered up at the lake last summer. It may be tied to a person who had a family member living here. I know you keep records of every person who visits a patient, since my mother is also a patient here. I'd like to take a look at who has visited a patient named Gerald Smith."

"Yes, the staff told me of your request. However, as I'm sure you can appreciate, our records, even those of visitors, are confidential. It's all part of the medical treatment process that we monitor all contacts of the patient. Many are emotionally compromised, as I'm sure you are aware. I would consider a release if you had a warrant, although I'm sure the corporate attorneys would have something to say about even that."

"Is there any other way, Doc? This is really important. But frankly, it's also a long shot. I don't know for certain that Mr. Smith's daughter is even alive, although I have reason to strongly suspect that she is. I also don't know for sure that she's been here, but that's what I need to know."

"Well, let me look," the doctor said, perusing Gerald Smith's chart. "Ah, yes, I see here that Mr. Smith has signed a power of attorney for health care decisions naming his son, Nathan, as the contact. Now, if the son ... "

"May I?" Angi said, as she reached across the physician's desk and picked up his phone. After a brief conversation, she handed the handset to the doctor.

"Well, it seems that Mr. Nathan Smith has given his permission for you to view the visitor records for his father," the doctor said when he hung up. "And yes, Janice Smith has visited, but she's only been here once — on June 27th of this year."

"Doc, please take my card and if Janice comes to visit again, would you or your staff call me right away. She may also use the name Henrietta Place. It's urgent that we talk to her."

Chapter 43

9:50 a.m. — September 20. It had been two weeks since the runaway girl in Portland had been reported as a Teach's latest possible victim. Angi had called the Portland Police Bureau two days earlier, but their attempts to locate a rental house that could be tied to Teach had proven fruitless. Neither had anyone spotted a car like Place's Mercury.

Angi couldn't dwell on a case with no current leads. She was, instead, walking through City Hall, headed for the Personnel Department. She needed to check on employment records for a former city employee who was suspected of assaulting a street vendor.

"Detective Masters!" someone shouted.

Angi turned toward the sound and saw Nathan Smith jogging across the foyer toward her.

"I was just going to call you when I saw you walk in," he said as he approached. "Janice called me out of the blue last night. She wouldn't tell me where she was, but I got the impression she's in town or close by. She asked about dad."

"Do you think she'll try to visit him?"

"Yeah, I think it's a good possibility."

"What about you? Will she come to see you?"

"No idea. I'd say it's more likely she'll try to see our dad."

"OK, thanks, Mr. Smith," Angi said. "Please let me know right away if you hear from her again."

"I will, Detective, but I have a feeling that I won't. Her voice sounded ... well, depressed. The way she said *good-bye* at the end of the call left me with a chill. It was like she was saying good-bye for the last time."

* * *

"She's going to visit her dad, Mike. I can feel it."

"From what you've told me, Angi, I have to agree," Garrison said. "But it also sounds like she's pretty off-balance. Confronting her in the care center could be dicey."

"Maybe we can take her outside. When she gets out of her car, or ..."

"Well, that would be less hazardous to the patients and we do know what her car looks like. At least if she hasn't changed cars."

"I don't think so. She seems to keep her distance from the actual crime scenes. I just feel like she thinks we don't know about her car, or at least not enough to pick it out."

"Alright. Set something up and let me know what you're planning."

"Will do, Boss," Angi said as she turned toward the door.

"And Angi ...?"

"Yeah, Boss."

"Let me know what you're planning *before* you do it, OK?'

* * *

Angi drove to a non-descript building in the warehouse district. Entering a building with a hand-painted sign listing the tenant as *SMC Cartage*, she went directly to a small office in the corner of the building. The building was the headquarters of the Vice and Intelligence Unit, the undercover arm of the Santa Rosa Police Department.

"Hey, Sarge," she said to Sergeant Rusty Collins, the unit supervisor, as she entered the office. "I need your help."

"My guys are always up for another Angela Masters extravaganza," Collins grinned.

"Come on, Sarge. That was *one* time — OK, maybe two."

"OK, guys. Gather around. Angi needs our help."

Angi gave the assembled undercover cops, who looked more like a gang of misfits and charlatans than highly trained detectives, a quick briefing on the Fire Storm case and its latest developments.

"So you think this woman will be coming to visit her father in the next couple of days?" one detective asked.

"Pretty good chance of it. My guess is that we can expect her probably today or tomorrow. The head doctor has my direct line and someone will be in the violent crimes office 24/7 monitoring the phone. He'll let us know when she shows up."

"What about this Teach guy? Will he be with her?" another detective asked.

"I can't say for sure, but probably yes. I just can't see them grabbing another girl here and that seems to be the only time Etta leaves Teach by himself. No, I think she's here just to see her father for what she seems to think might be the last time."

"OK, guys, I'll work out a rotating schedule so we can cover the parking lot around the clock with undercover cops. These are two nasty-assed killers and we will probably only have one chance. Angi, I'll give you a call when ..."

Collins was interrupted by the insistent ring of his telephone.

"For you, Angi," he said. "Everyone hold your position. This could be it."

"So much for planning," Angi said as she hung up the phone. "Janice just signed in to visit her father."

* * *

Nine detectives instantly scrambled for their unmarked cars, a mix of new luxury cars, 'beater' foreign sedans, and farm-ready pickup trucks. None were equipped with police emergency lights or sirens, a dead giveaway for an undercover operative. But the officers skillfully weaved their way through the late afternoon traffic, spurred by the knowledge that their target could leave at any time.

The first detective on the scene, driving a 1982 BMW which had been confiscated from a drug kingpin, cruised through the parking lot as if looking for the 'perfect' parking place for his shiny luxury car. After a couple of passes, he pulled the car into the center of two spaces.

Eyeing the less-fancy cars on either side of him, as a self-absorbed man of wealth might do, he keyed the radio microphone lying in his lap. Then he spoke in the enclosed car, "Subject vehicle is confirmed at my five o'clock, two rows back and four spaces from the street, facing away from the building. Male subject fitting Teach's description is seated in the front passenger seat."

He then left the car, glancing back as if to satisfy himself that his precious Beemer was safe occupying two parking spaces. He ambled toward the front door of the care center. His path would take him within a car-length of the parked Mercury.

Simultaneously, other undercover cars moved, one by one, into the lot. By chance, just as Collins pulled into the lot, the car parked next to the Mercury backed out and drove out of the lot. Collins steered his vehicle, a 1979 Ford F-150 pickup, with thoroughly oxidized and faded green paint job, toward the open space. As he pulled in, he maneuvered so that the dented left door was less than three feet from the passenger door of the Cougar.

As Angi and Devon, who had met her two blocks away, entered the front door of the facility, another detective spoke over the radio. "Inside team in place. Take him down! Go! Go!"

The 'wealthy' man suddenly bolted for the Mercury, jerking open the driver's door. He pointed his semi-automatic pistol at Teach and commanded, "Edward Teach, you're under arrest. Show your hands!"

Teach instead jerked the handle of his own door, thrusting it open and simultaneously dropping his right leg out. *Maybe I can get out of here with only a superficial wound, if this cop even shoots at all.*

As Teach's foot hit the pavement, Rusty Collins put the weight of his shoulder into opening the door of the Ford. The heavy pickup door smashed into the door of the Mercury, slamming it on Teach's right calf. The man's untamed moustache and chin whiskers snapped apart as he let out a bellowing scream.

"I said, 'show me your hands,' asshole!" the detective on the driver's side said.

Teach plopped both hands palm down on the dashboard. Seconds later, he was in handcuffs.

Chapter 44

3:17 p.m. — September 20. "Where is she, Doc?" Angi said as she and the undercover detective ran down the hall toward Gerald Smith's room.

"Out the back!" the doctor said, pointing toward the far end of the hall. "We were giving Mr. Smith a treatment and she had to wait in the visitor's lounge."

"Shit!" Angi said as she glanced briefly into the lounge. The window in Gerald Smith's room faced the inner courtyard, but the visitor's lounge, on the opposite side of the hallway, faced the parking lot. Janice had seen everything!

Angi and Devon sprinted for the back door. Devon hit the panic bar with such force that the door swung open and knocked two bricks loose from the outside wall when it hit. The homicide detectives stood in an employee parking lot behind the building. Guns in hand, they surveyed the lot and the wooded area beyond. Janice was nowhere to be seen.

Angi raised her portable radio to her lips. "Lock it down. Lock it down. No one leaves the parking lot!"

A marked patrol car, parked out of sight a block away, accelerated down the street, nearly hitting another car. Its driver then screeched to a stop, the car blocking the only opening from the street to the parking lot.

"Fucking reckless driver cops. That asshole should get a ticket!" Janice said from her position, lying in the back seat of the car nearly struck by the accelerating patrol unit. She peeked her head up to look briefly at the scene behind her and then turned back. As she had done twice before in the preceding 90 seconds, she poked the driver, a 26-year-old nurse, in the ribs and snarled, "Keep driving, bitch. And don't look at me!"

* * *

"Mr. Teach, I'm Detective Angela Masters," Angi said as she entered the interview room. The shaggy-bearded man was handcuffed to a steel table. The table itself was bolted to the floor, as was the steel bench the prisoner sat on.

"I remember you, Detective. You treated me nice, even after they arrested me. That don't happen too often."

"I'd like to ask you some questions, Mr. Teach. But first, I have to advise you of your rights."

"Sure, Detective, but you don't have to give me the whole spiel. I know I have a right to an attorney and don't gotta to talk to you. But I want to. So what do I need to sign?"

After Teach had acknowledged his *Miranda* rights on the department form, Angi said, "OK, Mr. Teach. I see from what I have here that your full name is Edward Lloyd Teach. You were born on July 23, 1950 in Killeen, Texas. Is that right?"

"Yes, ma'am. My father was a soldier — Army platoon sergeant — assigned to Fort Hood. Right after I was born, he was sent to Korea. He was there for a year. I guess my mom and I just stayed in Killeen during that time."

"And after your father came home?"

"We got transferred four or five times before I was 12 years old. Kentucky, Kansas, a while in South Carolina, I think. Germany. We were in Germany my whole 6th grade year."

"And your mother?"

"She never worked, at least as far as I remember. She was always home. There was just me and my mom and dad. I never had no brothers or sisters. My mom said one time that it hurt like hell having me and she never wanted to have another kid. 'Course, I don't think she knew I heard her, but it made me feel like shit, you know."

"Yeah. I can understand that. Tell me about your teen years."

"When I was like 14, my dad got out of the Army. Got his 20 years, you know. We were living in Salinas then, 'cause my dad was stationed at Fort Ord. Nothing special happened there. I mean I think I had an okay time in high school. It was always hard for me to make friends, maybe because we moved around so much when I was little. But I graduated from high school in Salinas in 1968."

"And did you go on to college from there?"

"Oh, no, ma'am. I graduated but I wasn't too good in school. Besides, it was pretty well ingrained in me that every man should do his time in the military. It was like a requirement of being an American, you know. At least, that's how my dad felt about it.

"So right out of high school, I joined the Navy. My dad was a little disappointed that I never went into the Army. But I think he understood that I was scared shitless of going to Vietnam and getting killed. The Navy seemed the safest way to go."

"What happened to you in the Navy?"

"After boot camp, I was supposed to go to sea. But something happened and I wound up on shore duty in Maine. Do you know how damned cold it gets in Maine? Anyway, there wasn't much to do there outside of work and sometimes me and my buddies would go into town to blow off some steam, you know.

"Well, this one day, we were at a bar in this little town. We was just minding our own business when these four townies started hassling us. We just tried to leave but they blocked our way — kept calling us war-mongers and baby-killers and shit like that. So this one guy was getting in my face and I just kind of lost it. I grabbed a pool cue from a table next to me and let him have it across the head. Knocked him out cold. The others took off after that."

"But you were court-martialed?"

"Yeah. I grew up in a family that was proud to serve our country. Then when I won't put up with a bunch of bullshit from a long-haired, hippie, draft-dodger, *I'm* the one who gets in trouble. They gave me the choice of a dishonorable discharge or two years in the brig. I left."

Angi couldn't help but stare at Teach's dirty long hair and wildly sprouting beard. *Long-haired hippie?* "So how did you wind up in California again? Did you come home to Salinas?"

"Oh, hell no! My dad would have disowned me if he knew I got kicked out of the Navy. But after I got shafted by the Navy, I didn't give a shit what he thought. Or what anyone else thought, for that matter. I was fed up with the whole military and its bullshit. I went to Mexico and signed on as a seaman on a tramp freighter operating out of Bucerias.

"In 1975, both my parents got killed by a drunk driver down by Coalinga. Probably just as well, 'cause I never wanted to see them again anyway. But after that, I just left the sea. I knocked around a while with odd jobs and got in a little trouble in a couple places. That was mostly for theft 'cause I didn't have no money and I needed to eat. I never did drugs or nothing like that."

"So how did you meet Jan ... I mean, Henrietta Place?"

"I was out looking for a good time — you know what I mean — and she was working the street in West Hollywood. While we were together, I mentioned that I had a thing for young girls. I always have but I never did nothing about it before. She told me she did too. She said that she would help me but I had to do like she said. So we joined up, and, well, that was it."

Chapter 45

5:40 p.m. — September 20. "Pull into this parking lot!" Janice said.

The petrified nurse did as she was told.

"Now give me your driver's license and don't get cute about any mace or anything like that in your purse!

"OK, I know your address, bitch. Get your ass on home and don't call the cops. Don't tell your mother or your boyfriend or your fucking dog about me. Because if the cops come after me, I'll come after you. And I think you can see that I'm pretty damned good at evading the cops."

The nurse nodded. Janice slammed the back door and disappeared around the corner of a nearby building.

Fifteen minutes later, the young nurse burst through the front door of her house. She took one look at her father, standing in the living room and staring wide-eyed at her abrupt entrance. The young woman immediately burst into tears and ran to her father's arms.

Minutes later, the on-duty watch commander, the lieutenant in charge of all field patrol operations in the city during his shift, pulled into a convenience store. The store chain had a policy of allowing on-duty emergency personnel to use the telephone in the back of the store. The dispatcher had instructed the lieutenant to call a certain person, and he had the number committed to memory.

"Captain Porter, this is John Lewis," the lieutenant said when the phone was answered.

"John, get some units over to the area of Guerneville and Burgundy asap. That bitch that Detective Masters is chasing kidnapped my daughter from her work and turned her loose in that area. I want that woman found!"

Patrol units searched through the night but were unable to locate the elusive Janice Smith.

* * *

"Let's move on to what you and Etta have been doing? How did you get started?" Angi said, continuing her interview of Teach.

"Abducting girls, you mean?"

"Yes."

"We went to this concert in Merced. I lived in Merced County for a little while one time, so I knew this place that has pretty good concerts. There was this girl there that looked like she was there all alone. Etta says, 'watch this. I'll get you a girl.'

"So Etta went over to the girl and started giving her what I call the mommy-treatment. You know, acting like she was concerned about the girl and everything. In just a little while, the girl was going with us."

"Here in Santa Rosa, you kept the girl in a rented house. Is that what happened in Merced?"

"No, we didn't think of that at first. We just took her to our motel room. It was one of those places where somebody screaming don't attract much attention if it don't last too long. We kept her tied and gagged, and I had her four or five times — you know."

Angi's training allowed her to suppress her true feelings about Teach's callous manner. She nodded as if 'having' a teen-aged girl numerous times was not at all shocking. "Go on."

"So that was about it. We kept her for a couple of days but then Etta said we would have to get rid of her so she wouldn't rat on us."

"What happened?"

"Etta told me to just strangle her while I was fu ... I mean while I was having sex with her. She would be all crying and everything and wouldn't see it coming. But I didn't do it so Etta jumped on the bed and strangled her. It was terrible."

"And then you dumped her body?"

"Yeah. That night, we put her in the trunk and took her to this place I knew outside of town and dumped her body in a creek. But her body must have washed up on the bank because I heard later on the news that somebody found her pretty quick."

"OK. You're doing really well, Ed. May I call you 'Ed?' "

Teach nodded.

"OK. So the detectives also found some little cut marks on the girl's breasts. Can you tell me about that?"

"That damn Etta is crazy, that's what! The girl would just be laying there tied up. We took her clothes so she wouldn't be running off if she happened to get loose. But she would just be laying there, and Etta had this knife. It was one of those hobby knives like you cut Styrofoam or something with. You know, with a metal handle and this really sharp blade that kind of looks like a triangle.

"So Etta goes up to her and lifts up her tit and makes this really long slow cut on the bottom. The girl was just freaking out but she couldn't go anywhere. But she did struggle around some. That just made Etta mad so she cut her some more. I really felt sorry for the poor kid."

But you didn't mind raping her, you sick son-of-a-bitch, Angi thought. "OK. Where did you go next?"

"San Luis Obispo. We did the same thing. Went to a concert and I picked out a girl that I liked that seemed like she was alone. Etta chatted her up but that time, Etta told her that I was a Navy hero and that she would be safe with me. The girl believed her and she walked out with me, no problems."

"But that time, you had rented a house."

"Yeah. We decided there was too much chance of someone noticing us at a motel. Plus, we couldn't really keep the girl a long time because someone would be coming around to check on the room. So I had just got some phony IDs — well, I ain't saying where 'cause it don't matter. I got them right before that to write checks with, but I used one of them to rent this old house.

"I paid cash for it so we couldn't be traced. But Etta was scared to stay there anyway if we were keeping the girl for a long time. She got a motel room someplace and just came around when she wanted to have fun with the kid."

"And what do you mean by 'have fun'?"

"Like I said. Cut her. She never really cut the girl deep, but she knew those sharp little cuts hurt like hell. Truth was, after that, I was always scared that if I pissed her off, I might wake up with her cutting on me."

"Do you know why Etta cut them like that?"

"Just to get her kicks, I guess. I never asked, 'cause like I said, I didn't want her cutting me."

"OK. Go on."

"So we kept the kid chained up in the basement of this house. I put some canvas that I found on the windows so nobody could look in, 'cause I was living there too, even though the girl was tied up in the basement."

Angi nodded again but didn't speak. *I don't want to break Teach's train of thought. Plus, I don't want to screw up the whole interview by pulling the balisong from my purse and castrating this bastard right here in the interview room. So I've got to keep my cool.*

"So after a week or so, we strangled her and dumped her body in an old freezer that was left in the house."

"OK, where did you go next?"

"Right here. Santa Rosa."

Chapter 46

8:20 p.m. – September 20. "Would you like to take a break, Mr. Teach?" Angi asked. "I can have some food brought in for you."

"A beer would be nice." The hairy lips parted in a rotted-tooth smile.

"How about maybe a soft drink or water?" Angi didn't smile, but she didn't berate the man for his feeble attempt at humor. She needed him to trust her just a little longer.

"Water is good. And maybe a hamburger with onions and ketchup?"

"I'll see what I can do. You need the restroom or anything?"

Teach shook his head.

"OK, sit right here and I'll be back."

"I'll just do that," the man said, rattling the handcuff against the metal ring welded to the steel table, as he managed a weak smile.

As Angi stepped out of the room, Officer Rapacon approached her. "Can I ask a question, Detective?"

"Sure."

"I was watching your interview from the viewing room. How did you get him to roll over so easily? I mean, this guy is involved in a bunch of felonies."

Angi smiled at the young officer. "Well, I have to admit that he is spilling his guts a whole lot easier than most. But you should never rule out the idea that your suspect is an idiot. By that I mean that crooks don't always behave like you and I might expect."

Rapacon nodded.

"But in this case, my gut tells me that Teach was in over his head. He's scared and he sees cooperation as his only way to help himself. And I also think he's afraid of Place."

"Thank you, Detective. I've got a lot to learn," the officer said.

A few minutes later, Angi returned to the interview room with a plastic cup filled with water. "I ordered your hamburger, and some fries too. It should be here in a little while."

"Thank you, Detective." The smile breaking through the twisted whiskers was genuine.

Angi nodded. "So, Mr. Teach, you were telling me about coming to Santa Rosa."

"Huh?" The man's mind was on the hamburger. "Oh, yeah. So after we left down there, Etta said she wanted to make a stop in Santa Rosa. I asked her why she wanted to stop there — here — but she didn't say.

"So we got here and she dropped me off, just like before, and I rented a house. Then Etta picked me up a while later and dropped me off near where the house was so I could get it ready."

"And what did you do to 'get it ready'?"

"Well, the mattress thing in the basement had worked pretty well in San Luis Obispo so I was going to do the same setup here. The house wasn't furnished, but there was an old mattress in the corner of the basement. And there was some chain and a rope. You know, like lots of people have those around for just in case. So I had what we needed to hold the girl. There was a refrigerator and there was a plastic table and chairs — you know, picnic stuff — in the basement too. That was really all I needed."

"Where did you get the cuff thing that was on the chain?"

"Oh, that!" Teach chuckled. "I had two of those from an old set of leg-irons that I found on one of the merchant ships I was on. I cut the chain that was between the cuffs and used one in San Luis and the other one here. I meant to take the one from here for the next place, but it was kind of crazy and ..."

Teach stared at the blank interview room wall. His mind suddenly filled with the horrific images from the basement — the blood, the screaming, the smell of death. *How much should I tell her? She seems nice but she's still a detective and I know I'm going to jail.*

Angi broke his trance. "Yes. Tell me about what happened."

Teach hesitated. *I've never experienced anything like that in my life, and I never want to again. Can I trust her? I'm going to jail, sure as the tide, but for how long? Will it help me to tell the whole story?*

"Everything was going just like before. Etta hit up this girl at a concert and then we brought her to the house. She thought Etta was some kind of social worker so she didn't give us no trouble.

"She was a little scared of me, but Etta told her that I looked rough so I could handle anybody who messed with runaway girls we were trying to help. Etta was pretty proud of that line.

"The first time the girl knew she was in trouble was when we got to the house. She didn't want to go to the basement, but Etta just pushed her down the stairs. She got bruised up from that but didn't break nothing. Then we chained her up and stripped her and I had sex with her a couple of times. And Etta cut her a few times, like before."

"Did she resist?" *Why was this one different? Why did they cut her up so bad? Did she fight them?*

"No more than usual. A little wiggling, you know, trying to keep me out of her but then she gave in. But then Etta was gone for a couple of days and I was getting worried. I just left the girl alone and kind of hung out in the house. I was worried that Etta had run off and stuck me with getting caught with the girl."

"Did you ever think of just letting her go?"

"Yeah, I did. In fact, I was gonna do that if Etta didn't come back in a day or so. But I had to figure out how to get away first. I didn't have no car or nothing. But every time I went outside to try to scope out the area and figure where I could grab a car, this nosy bitch in the house next door would be outside and try to talk to me. I was afraid she would remember what I looked like."

There was a knock on the interview room door. "Looks like your hamburger is here," Angi said. "We'll continue after you have a chance to eat."

* * *

Janice spent the night huddled on a heated exhaust grate in an alley in the downtown area. *I haven't had to do this since, damn, I don't remember when. The cops have Teach, who has probably already spilled his guts about the motel where we were staying so I can't go there. And they have my car. Until I can boost another one, I'm stuck here.*

She pulled the tattered shipping blanket that she had found in a dumpster closer around her shoulders.

Janice, you'll never have to come back to this rat-hole Santa Rosa. That's what I said to myself in 1967 when Ben took me away. And now, where am I? In a rat-infested alley in a rat-hole city. This is all Teach's fault, but I need him if I'm going to get out of this. Besides, I'm kind of sweet on the son-of-a-bitch.

She slept fitfully. Her mind swirled with thoughts of how she would spring Teach from custody. She was also aware of every sound in the alley. Any footfall or a car engine could be a cop checking the alley. *Catching the infamous Henrietta Place would make that cop a hero,* she told herself.

The following morning, she slipped out of the alley just as the sun was peeking over the Mayacamas ridge. She hoped the newspaper she found in a business's doorway would give some account of Teach's capture. Although the cops would not likely release what, if anything, Teach told them, they would have to tell the press when he was to be in court. *That will be my chance.*

Chapter 47

9:55 p.m. — September 20. "Hope I didn't interrupt your train of thought, Angi," Julie said when Angi left Teach in the interview room with his hamburger and water. "From what I heard on the monitor, it sounded like a good stopping place."

"No, it's fine, Jules. It was a good breaking point before he gets into what happened that night. And stopping to let him eat should help ease his mind to keep talking."

The detectives watched their suspect through a one-way mirror. "He acts like he doesn't have a care in the world. Just sits there eating his burger," Julie said.

"Yeah, I'm not sure he really gets how much trouble he's in," Angi said, "and I want to keep it that way for now."

Teach finished the last morsel of ground beef, licking the paper plate clean of even the grease left by the meat. Then he pushed the paper plate away, took a long drink of water, and sat staring at the wall.

"Get enough?" Angi asked pleasantly as she entered the room.

"Yes, ma'am. That was great. Thank you."

"OK, Mr. Teach. Now, you were talking about getting some phony IDs from Ned Low."

"I never told you that. How did you know?"

"You told me — just now."

Teach grinned. "You are good, lady."

"OK, so then we were talking about you being in the house and thinking about letting Abby go. You did know that her name was Abby, didn't you?"

Teach nodded. "Yes, ma'am. She told me her name when we were just talking while I was figuring what to do with her."

"What happened next?"

"Well, this one night, like on the second day that Etta was gone, I was just wandering around the house, trying to figure what to do. I was rummaging around in the basement and I found this really cool Japanese sword. It wasn't the big long one like the Samurais carried — you know, the ones they use to cut your head off like in *Shogun*. Did you see *Shogun*, Detective? It was a really cool movie."

"Yes, I did. So what did you do with the sword?"

* * *

Julie, listening on a monitor on the other side of the one-way glass, thumbed through the case file and then picked up the telephone.

"Mr. Kalder?" she said when a man answered the phone. "This is Detective Julie Phelps in Santa Rosa. We have a man in custody for the murder that happened in the house you own here. He told us he found a Japanese sword in the basement. I'm trying to confirm if that might be true."

"Oh, my God! Did he use my *wakizashi* to kill that poor girl?"

"We don't know that, sir. He just told my partner that he found it in the basement. At this point, I'm just trying to confirm if he's telling the truth."

"Yeah, probably so. The movers were supposed to bring both swords, a *katana* and a *wakizashi*. Those are the two swords worn by Samurai. When we were unpacking here in Arizona, I noticed that I only had the *katana*. I wasn't too worried because I knew I had probably left it on the back of a bench in the basement. I just figured I would get it next time we were in Santa Rosa. Are you sure he didn't use it to hurt that girl?"

"He hasn't said that, sir. Thank you. I'll let you know if we need anything else." Julie wanted to turn her attention back to the story unfolding in the interview room.

* * *

"Nothing. I didn't hurt the girl with it, if that's what you're asking."

"OK, Mr. Teach. I just need to know what happened to Abby. If you didn't hurt her, how did it happen?"

"It wasn't me. It wasn't. I was just looking over the sword 'cause it was cool to think about being a Samurai or some kind of pirate like they had in *Shogun*. That's when Etta came in."

"What time was that?"

"I don't have no watch, but I'd guess it was midnight or a little after. Etta came back said, 'where's my girl? Is she ready for a good time?' She started downstairs when she saw the sword in my hand. She grabbed it out of my hand and pulled it out of its holster or whatever you call it. I was sick because I could tell from the look on her face that she was going to use it on Abby."

That's the first time he's used her name. He's starting to empathize with the victim. That's a giant step forward, Angi thought.

"So Etta went downstairs and stood over Abby. She was laying on the mattress and crying. Etta pulled out this strap-on that she had got somewhere. I'd never seen it before, but she kind of dangled it in front of the girl and said, 'now I'm gonna have you too.' And then she showed the sword to her and said, 'and don't fight me, bitch, or I'll cut you really good with this.' "

"So then Etta raped her with the strap-on. Then she said, 'now it's time for the pole. Won't that be fun?' And she unlocked the leg iron so she could move Abby to the pole to tie her up there."

"And what was the purpose of that?"

"So she couldn't move while Etta sliced on her tits some more, I guess. That's what she really liked to do."

"And what were you doing?"

"I was just standing back. I didn't even want to watch because it made me sick when she would cut them like that. I sort of started to go upstairs but Etta said she would slit my dick with that knife if I tried to leave. And I believed her."

"So then what happened?"

"As Etta was moving Abby to the pole, Abby kicked her real hard. If Etta was a man, she woulda been down for the count." Teach smiled at the thought.

"So then Abby just bolted up the stairs. She didn't care that she was naked. She was just moving outta there. But Etta managed to take a swipe at her with the sword. She cut her shoulder and maybe part of her arm. Anyway, Abby screamed and I saw her grab her shoulder but she kept running."

"Did you try to stop her?

"Not at first. I mean, I knew if she got away, I would be in trouble. But it took me a minute to realize what was going on, I guess. Anyway, Etta yelled at me and then we both ran after her.

"She was running around the neighborhood and screaming for help. Then she ran up to this one house and started banging on the door, but I guess everyone was asleep. When she did that, Etta caught up with her. She started to pull her away, but Abby broke loose and ran across the street.

"I caught up with her and tackled her into some bushes. But she wiggled free and banged on the window of this house. I was still on the ground when Etta ran past me. Then I heard the most awfulest scream I have ever heard."

"Do you know what happened?"

"I didn't right then, but Etta told me later. She said that she took a swipe at the girl with the sword. Abby put her hand up, like to defend herself, and Etta just sliced her hand clean off. Still, Abby took off running again but I guess she was getting weak, because we caught her and dragged her back to the house.

"As soon as we got her back to the basement, Etta just went out of her mind. She stabbed Abby in the chest and it was obvious she was dead. Then Etta told me to find a garbage bag, and she just started cutting Abby's body up right there on the floor."

"So you put the parts of her body in the bag?"

"Yeah, except for her hand. Etta said we had to make sure to get rid of it separately because her prints might be on file. At first, she said we should go out and find the other hand too. I didn't want to and then she decided it would be too risky anyway if maybe someone heard Abby screaming and called the cops.

"So we just put everything in the bag, except the torso. It wouldn't fit so we snuck it out to Etta's car. Then we took it all up to this bridge that Etta knew about and tossed everything over. Etta said it would all sink in the lake and that nobody would ever find it."

"Was the head in the bag too?"

"Oh, yeah. I forgot about that. Yeah, it was at first, but then when we were taking the bag outside, I looked over and saw that bitch's house next door — the one who kept bugging me when I would go out. So I decided to give her a little present. I took the head out of the bag and tossed it onto her roof." Teach chuckled lowly.

Shit, this guy acts like it was a junior-high prank pulled on someone he didn't like at school.

"I never told Etta until later, and damn, was she pissed."

"What happened next?"

"Nothing much. We cleaned up a little in this all night gas station, then went and got some breakfast. After that, we just took off. I thought we were headed south somewhere but we wound up over in Reno."

Chapter 48

11:27 p.m. — September 20. "Sorry to bother you so late, Mike, but I thought you should know about this." Angi described Teach's statement to her supervisor, pausing only for Garrison's occasional 'oh, shit' and 'that sick bastard' comments.

"I think we should alert the fire department's dive team in the morning to go up to the lake and see if they can find the sword. Teach says they threw it off the bridge too. It wasn't on the jetty with the torso, so it must have gone into the water."

"What about the other hand?"

"Probably gone. Teach said they threw it off another bridge on their way to Reno. From his description, I think he's talking about the bridge over Mare Island Strait on Highway 37. If that's the case, it's in the strait and we'll never find it."

"So he's in the county jail now?"

"Yep. Safe and secure until his arraignment on Monday."

"And you have his waiver locked down tight?"

"Absolutely. I'm sure Chuck Teska, or whoever shows up at the arraignment from the public defender's office, will argue that his confession wasn't voluntary. But it's all on tape and I re-admonished him after every break.

"In fact — and this is on tape — he actually got mad after about the third time of me reminding him that he could have a lawyer. He said something like 'no bottom-feeding shyster lawyer can help me now. Only thing I got going for me is to tell the truth.'"

"Teska will like that," Garrison smiled.

"So now we just have to find Janice Smith, or Etta Place as she calls herself now. I don't think that will be easy."

* * *

Janice had been huddled under a flat-bed semi-trailer across the street from the seedy motel for nearly six hours. Her legs were cramping and she had to pee. In that time, she had seen nothing that caused her to think the cops were onto their hideout. Maybe Teach hadn't told them about it after all. But what else had he told them?

I remember Angela Masters from high school. She made nice to everybody but she was still one of the 'goodie girls.' Her and those fucking Amazons on the volleyball team. Thought they were all cool because they had long legs and blonde ponytails. Of course, they would never have let someone like me onto their dumbass team, even if I had tried out for it.

Janice checked her five-dollar digital watch. 2:14 a.m. *Who gives a fuck if it's 2:14 or 2:16? Isn't 'about 2:15' close enough?*

Cautiously, she crept from her hiding place. She moved slowly and stiffly, eyeballing in every direction, looking for any sign of an undercover car with a cop staking out the motel. *Damn! After all the bad luck in the past couple of months, Reno and then San Bernardino, maybe I'm getting a break for a change.*

Five minutes later, she stood on the second floor balcony of the motel, pressing herself into a corner near the stairs for one last look around before she committed to the room. *What if some cop is staked out in the room, waiting for me? Shit, I can't worry about everything. Plus, the room has been dark since sundown. There can't be anyone in there. I hope.*

Carefully, but trying to move normally so as not to call attention to herself, Janice approached room 209. Taking one more look around, she inserted the key in the knob and pushed the door open.

* * *

Angi groaned as she opened her eyes, the incessant jangle of the telephone in her ears. *2:20 a.m. Oh, shit. Not a call-out, please. I just got to bed an hour ago.*

"Angi, it's Devon."

"Yeah, Devon. I'm awake, sort of. What we got?"

"No call-out, if that's what you mean. But I got some news that I thought you'd want to know. Dispatch paged me a little while ago with a message to call the detective in Portland. The message said there was no hurry, but I figured if he had just called, he was probably still at his office. So I called up there."

"About the missing girl?"

"Yeah. I had left him a message yesterday while you were in the interview room that we had Teach is custody. He was calling back to tell me that the girl had come home unharmed last night. She was at some girlfriend's house until she cooled off about the beef with her parents.

"Apparently, she told the friend's parents that her parents were out of town. They didn't think much of it because she had stayed with them before when the parents both had to travel for their work. The detective didn't say anything about the bearded guy that was with her in the video, but this doesn't look like Teach's and Place's work."

"I don't think so either. I asked him about the girl in Portland and he denied that they had anything to do with it. So I guess I'll chalk that one up in the 'believe Teach' column."

"So you believe his story?"

"At least most of what he told me seemed pretty believable. I have to tell you that even though Teach is one scary-looking dude, I think Janice is the real predator of the pair. He responds more like a 12-year-old and I just don't see him putting all this together."

"And she's the one in the wind. Do you think she'll try to spring Teach?"

"Hell, why should she? What does he have that she needs? She tried to see her father. That seems to be the only thing she came back to Santa Rosa to do. She won't go back to the care center now that she knows we're on to her. My guess is that she's on the road to as far away from here as she can get."

Chapter 49

2:37 a.m. — September 21. Janice pushed the door open and stepped back against the railing of the second story walkway. She was ready to bolt in either direction if a cop suddenly appeared in the motel room. But nothing happened.

Cautiously, she reached inside the open door and flicked a light switch. The lone lamp in the room came on, its dim bulb casting soft shadows across the sparse furnishings. *At least I know there's no one under the bed.*

Two days before, she and Teach had discovered that the bed's broken down mattress sat not on box springs, but on a sheet of plywood. The plywood deck was elevated off the floor by a simple plywood box. But the box itself, when the mattress and deck were removed, was a perfect hiding place. It wasn't a hiding place a cop wanting to spring up to arrest her would use, but for other things ...

Leaving the front door open as an escape route, she moved cautiously to the bathroom and flicked on the light there. After a few moments of popping and flickering, the ballast of the florescent light over the sink finally energized the neon gas to glow faintly. *No one here either.*

She looked around the outside area once again and then pushed the front door closed. She turned to the bed and flipped the mattress and plywood deck onto the floor. *Good. They're still there.*

Lying on the filthy carpet inside the plywood box was a 9mm Beretta pistol and two bundles of cash wrapped with rubber bands. The money, about $800, had come from cashing two bogus cashiers' checks in Redding a few days before.

Stuffing the gun in her elastic waistband and one bundle of cash in her coat pocket, she stared at the mattress. *God, I would love to lay down, just for a little while. I'm so damned tired.*

But then reality set in. Sooner or later, the cops would find out about this place. She had been lucky to far. Now was not the time to get stupid, even if the thin mattress was far more inviting than an exhaust grate in some alley.

* * *

That damned phone! It seemed like no more than a few minutes had passed since Devon's early morning call, but then Angi noticed the sliver of sunlight cutting through a small gap in her bedroom curtains.

"Angi, this is your Uncle Dave. Are you awake?"

"Hi, Uncle Dave. I wasn't but ..." The clock said 10:34. *I don't ever remember sleeping this late.*

"Sorry to wake you, princess, but I thought you'd want to know. Our divers found the Samurai sword in the lake below the bridge, just where your perp said it would be."

"Your divers? I thought the fire department ..."

"Jurisdictional thing. But your weapon is safe and sound. Of course, there are no prints or blood on it. It's been in the water quite a while. But at least it corroborates that part of the story you got, at least from what Mike Garrison told me."

"Yeah, it does. Do you have it with you? I can come out ..."

"No, stay home. You need the rest. I have the deputy who found it taking it in to the PD's evidence locker right now. That way, it cuts down on the chain of custody too."

* * *

At the same time, Janice was waking to the same sunlight. But her 'bedroom' had no curtains, and she had no blanket. At least the branches of the fir tree she was huddled under protected her from the morning dew. The tree was a perfect location. It had a broad canopy and was trimmed just high enough above the ground to allow the groundskeeper's mower blades to pass unimpeded in the summer. It was also the only tree for 100 feet around in the northwest corner of the Annadel State Park.

The park offered the advantage of having no vehicle accesses. Cops weren't likely to leave their cars in the nearby residential areas to walk through the park unless they got a call there. Janice had grown up in a house less than one-half mile from her current hiding place and she didn't remember ever seeing cops walk around in the area.

Brushing the dead fir needles from her clothes, Janice moved slowly out of Annadel and through the connected parks of Spring Lake and Howarth. She had once worked at a fast food joint not far from Howarth on the Sonoma Highway.

If there were no cop cars there, she would get some food to go, and then disappear back into the huge state park. The chance of anyone she worked with still being at the restaurant was too remote to even consider, given the turnover in the fast food industry. Still, she decided she would linger a while before entering.

An hour later, she returned to the fir tree, happily convinced that no one had recognized her. She had enough food to last for the weekend if she was frugal. *No way I can go back to that restaurant, just in case.* Sure the food would be cold, but by Monday, she would be well on her way to someplace far away, where she could again enjoy life. Life, and hot food, and a warm bed, and Teach.

Teach is not the brightest fish in the sea, but he's the only guy who ever treated me nice. Well, besides that nerdy kid in high school, Roger something-or-other. But he was popular in his own way, never moving with the 'in' crowd but still not hated by them. Not like me, a nobody to all those popular chickies with their bouffant hair and prissy attitudes.

I never expected to see him in that shoe store that day, but I recognized him right off. I figured I had to say something to him, because it was obvious that he recognized me too. It was nice to talk to him, and he was as nice as ever to me. But even though he was nice to me in high school, I knew then that nothing would ever happen because Roger was smitten with Angela Masters.

Angela Masters! Detective Angela Masters. Maybe I should get Teach to help me grab her. Then we could haul her away in the trunk to someplace where I could carve little designs on her tits. Damn, that would be fun!

Her smile disappeared almost as soon as it had arrived and the vision collapsed in a realization. Masters carried a gun. From what Janice had heard, she was pretty good with it. *No sense being stupid, no matter how appealing it sounds. Nope. Just stick with your plan. And then you can go back to being Etta and leave that loser Janice behind once and for all.*

Chapter 50

8:40 a.m. — September 23. "Kim, you're here early," Angi said as she brewed a cup of Earl Grey tea at the sink in the corner of the detective's work area. Devon had been the first detective in the office that morning. As the first one in, he had made a pot of coffee, but Angi avoided police station coffee at nearly all costs.

"I wanted to get a start on that Mercury you got Friday night," the lab technician said.

"Oh, yeah. Janice, er ... Etta's, car. Did you find anything?"

"Yeah. I found prints from both the woman and Teach, and she was driving last. No surprises there, but I think you'll like this," she said, handing a scrap of paper to Masters.

"OK. This is the address of the care facility where we caught Teach. I know the address well. My mother is there, too. Remember?"

"Turn it over, Angi."

"Oh, my God!"

"That's the address of that fleabag motel ..."

"Yeah, I know what it is. It's just the kind of place I would expect them to hole up. Great work, Kim!"

Angi grabbed her jacket and purse and yelled across the room. "Devon, let's go for a ride. I'll brief you on the way."

* * *

Two hours earlier, Janice had moved from the fir tree that had been her home and shelter for the previous two nights. It was 30 minutes before sunrise but already, the residential areas to the west of Annadel Park were stirring. Still, there were few people out on the street. No one seemed to take notice of the disheveled woman who moved deliberately along the sidewalk.

Two blocks over is the house where I grew up. Maybe I ... No. She put the notion out of her head. She had driven by it last summer, but now was not the time for nostalgia. It was the time for action and everything had to be timed just right.

Ahead, an older Toyota idled in a driveway. *Who needs to warm their car when the temperature is in the lower 50's? Hell, I slept in this weather last night without a blanket and this asshole is wasting gas. Maybe he just wanted it to be available for me.* Janice grinned and quickly looked around.

Within seconds, she had backed the Toyota out of the driveway and had disappeared into the traffic on Summerfield Road. A few minutes later, she pulled the Toyota behind an abandoned Union 76 station. There she changed the license plates to a pair she had stolen from another car the night before.

It wouldn't take the cops too long to put the two thefts together. However, Janice was confident that by the time they figured out what car and license number to look for, they would have far bigger things to worry about.

* * *

"OK, Teach. It's time to go," the jail deputy said. "We're going to take a little ride to court." It was barely a quarter mile from the jail to the courthouse, but no one would ever consider walking the prisoner down the sidewalk for his arraignment on the kidnapping and murder charges.

A marked sheriff's car was parked next to the back door of the jail. Teach, his hands cuffed behind his back, was escorted to the car by two deputies. Neither had seen the Toyota idling in the parking lot fifty feet away.

As the deputies opened the back door of the cruiser to load their prisoner, two shots rang out and both deputies fell to the ground.

"Run, Teach! You son-of-a-bitch! Run! Here!"

Teach couldn't believe his eyes. There was Etta, frantically motioning him toward a car he didn't recognize. He hesitated for a moment, not sure he really wanted to go with the crazy woman. But then he ran with all his might. It took a few moments for other officers to learn what had happened. By then, the Toyota was fleeing south through the city.

* * *

"All units, stand-by," the dispatcher broadcast. "Felony suspect Edward Teach just escaped from custody outside the county jail. Possibly accompanied by female, Janice Smith, aka Etta Place. Subjects last seen headed south on Mendocino in a green Toyota. Units be advised, three shots fired at the SO by the female. Two deputies are down. Injuries are reported to be non-life-threatening."

The city air was suddenly alive with the sound of sirens. It didn't take long to locate the fleeing car.

"Santa Rosa, Lincoln 13," an officer broadcast. "I'm in pursuit of the suspect vehicle southbound on Mendocino approaching College."

Devon, driving to the motel where Janice might have been staying, immediately turned his car while Angi activated the lights and siren.

Julie Phelps was on her way to an interview on another case when the emergency broadcast came out. She listened as unit L13, still pursuing the Toyota, broadcast his location and direction.

Stay on Mendocino, asshole, and you're mine!, she thought.

"Lincoln 13, continuing south on Mendocino past College."

As the Toyota approached Seventh Street, Julie accelerated her car. Her timing was perfect. She t-boned the fleeing Toyota in the intersection of Seventh and Mendocino, sending the small car spinning into a light pole on the corner.

"Lincoln 13, a detective unit has terminated the pursuit at Seventh and Mendocino. Suspects are on foot, running south on Mendocino."

"Perfect!" Devon said as he power-slid his car into the intersection of Fifth and Mendocino. It was like a scene from a movie as the two fugitives bounced against the side of the unmarked police car.

The pair picked themselves up as Angi jumped from the passenger side. She saw Julie closing fast behind them.

Well, I know what the third shot was, Angi thought. Teach's handcuffs dangled from his wrists, but the connecting chain had been broken, probably by the force of a bullet.

Chapter 51

9:32 a.m. — September 23. The two criminals ran, cutting a zig-zag course to avoid being hit by any shots the detectives might fire. Angi and Julie sprinted after them, unspoken communication saying that if the pair split up, Angi would follow Smith and Julie would take Teach. Devon and several uniformed officers roared down the city's streets, trying to position their cars ahead of the fleeing killers.

Angi was still in nearly the same good physical condition as she had been as a college athlete years before. She began to gain on the pair as she rounded a corner. Suddenly, she fell to the ground grimacing in pain and cussing like a sailor. She had stepped on a nail protruding from a board in the littered alley.

Julie slowed to help her, but Angi motioned her forward. "Go! Go! I'll be okay," she said.

As Julie disappeared around a corner where the alley intersected the next street, Angi gritted her teeth and pulled the nail from her foot. At that moment, Devon's car came to a stop in a screeching slide near her. Angi hobbled to the car as fast as she could and climbed into the passenger seat. "Go!" she commanded before she had closed the door.

No one spoke on the radio. Every officer listened as Julie, her labored breathing pounding into the portable radio, broadcast updates of her location and direction. Police units maneuvered to cut off the fleeing felons.

Janice and Teach rounded a corner to see two marked police cars obstructing their getaway path, less than a block ahead. Janice started to turn back, but spotted a dark-haired female detective rapidly approaching on foot, her Smith and Wesson .45 in her hand. Just behind the detective, an unmarked car approached, its siren wailing. Janice recognized Angela Masters in the passenger seat.

The two killers stood in the street, their eyes darting in search of an escape. Suddenly, a woman walked out of a store, a mere ten feet from where the fugitives stood. The woman, intent on directing the two small children who were each holding her hand, was oblivious to the events going on in front of her eyes. That was until Janice Smith grabbed her around the throat and held a gun to her head.

"Lose the kiddies, bitch, or they die!"

Suddenly realizing what was happening, the woman shook her hands away from the children. Then she screamed, "Run! Run to the police car, kids! Go now!" The frightened youngsters ran into the waiting arms of a uniformed officer, who whisked them to safety.

Janice pulled the woman close to her, the gun at the woman's right temple. Her own head was shielded behind the unfortunate hostage's head. She backed toward a large inset doorway, dragging her unwilling companion close behind. Teach moved with her, exposed to the police and eyeing their every move.

Devon swerved the car to a stop, facing the fugitives. He and Angi quickly left the vehicle and positioned themselves behind the open front doors. Julie ducked behind a parked car and trained her gun on Teach.

"Back off, pigs. Especially you, Masters. Don't get cute or I'll kill this bitch."

"Everyone hold your fire!" Angi said. "She's too close to the hostage for a shot." The pain in her foot was now forgotten in the rush of adrenaline. *If I can just keep her in one spot until SWAT can get some snipers up on the roofs to take a shot ...*

"Teach! Janice! You don't want it to end like this. Give it up and no one will harm you," Angi yelled.

"Back off!" Smith said in reply. "You need to be thinking of a way to get us outta here with no cops following us. Get me a helicopter or something!"

"Etta," Teach hissed. "We're trapped here. The door behind us is locked. If they get a sniper with a scope up on a roof, he'll just pick us off. Let's give up. It's over."

"Bullshit, Teach. You weasel. I should have known I couldn't count on you."

Janice warily eyed the rooftop across the street. She saw no signs of a sniper. Still, she pulled her hostage closer, moving her head further behind the woman's until only her right eye peeked past the woman's hair.

"Masters! Don't think you can get a sniper on me. I have my finger on the trigger. Even if I get shot, I can still pull the trigger and blow this bitch's head up like a melon."

"No one is going to shoot, Janice," Angi said. "Everyone! Hold your fire," she yelled again to the assembled officers.

Come on. Where is that sniper? And, God, I hope he sees that she has her finger on the trigger. She might kill this hostage merely by reaction if she's shot. He'll just have to wait for an opportunity. Angi's mind reeled to come up with options.

"Etta," Teach pleaded. "Come on. Let's give it up. I know a good lawyer."

She didn't answer. Teach looked woefully at Smith, and then raised his hands.

"Walk this way, Teach," Devon yelled. "No one will ..."

In one fast and fluid motion, Janice moved her gun from the hostage's head and fired one shot. The bullet penetrated Teach's neck and severed his spine at the base of his skull. As his body dropped to the ground, her gun flew back under the hostage's chin.

"Hold your fire! Hold your fire!" Angi yelled to the officers.

"Smart move, Masters! Now ba ..."

Blam! One shot rang out from Angi's left. Angi couldn't see it but the .45 caliber hollowpoint round passed less than an inch from the hostage's ear at more than 600 miles per hour. The hot lead singed a brown streak in her hair as it screamed by.

A micro-second later, the bullet crashed squarely into Janice's right eye. The mushrooming projectile instantly carried a large part of her brain with it as it exited the back of her head through a four inch wide hole. The hostage screamed as the red-haired killer, dead while she still stood, fell to the ground with a dull thud. Her finger was still in the trigger guard when her hand hit the pavement.

"Can't pull a trigger with no brain to tell your finger to do it," Anderson said calmly.

"Devon?!"

"Since the lobby deal, I've been practicing a lot on my own. That and a tense situation will do wonders for reviving the muscle memory already developed as a marksman."

The 'best shooter on the department' was back.

Angi, Devon, and Julie, with half-a-dozen uniformed officers, moved forward, their guns at the ready. But the fugitives were not going to move, ever. A uniformed officer escorted the shaken hostage away to reunite with her children.

Angi turned to her partner and smiled. "Good job, Devon."

Then her smile faded and she stared down at the fallen criminals with disdain. *This came too late for Abby. And it's too late for the girls in Merced and San Luis Obispo. Maybe this will give closure to the girls in Reno and San Bernardino, but probably not. There will always be predators like you out there, looking to take advantage of runaway girls, and even boys.*

But one thing is damn sure. You two assholes will never hurt anybody again.

She turned to walk away — and her smile returned.

Thank you

Thank you for your purchase. I hope you enjoyed this book.

I would sincerely appreciate your review on Amazon.com. Reviews help an author produce content that readers would like to see.

Are you on my mailing list yet? If not, please follow the link below (or type it into your browser) to sign up. You will hear about new releases, get the inside track on the development of each new book, and be eligible for occasional special offers such as giveaways, advance reader copies, and special pricing on individual books and sets only offered to subscribers.

www.mikeworleybooks.com/subscribe

About the Author

Mike Worley is a veteran of 34 years in law enforcement, moving through the ranks from Police Officer to Captain with the Boise, ID Police Department. During his career, he served as an investigative commander in both criminal investigations and internal affairs. He then accepted a position as Chief of Police with the suburban Meridian, ID Police Department.

Following his retirement from active policing, he continued his law enforcement involvement as an instructor and course coordinator for a university-based police training facility. He has also consulted nationally on police policy issues.

He is retired and lives with his wife, Nancy, in Louisville, KY.

Acknowledgements

From a story idea suggested by
Detective Dave Smith

My thanks to the following people who provided
editorial comment:

Members of the Stuffed Owls Writers Group of Louisville
and
Jennie Armento, Amanda Beam, Thonie Hevron,
Steve Leonard, Ken Malgren, Wade Spain,
Waights Taylor and Cheryl Worthey

I would also like to thank Manager Brenda Johnson and
the staff of Starbucks Store 2571 at Hurstbourne & Shelbyville
Roads, Louisville, KY for their hospitality. The majority of this
book was written in their store.

Other books by Mike Worley

"Retribution – An Angela Masters Detective Novel"

"Grand Jeté – An Angela Masters Detective Novel"

"Entitlement – An Angela Masters Detective Novel"

"Ghost – An Angela Masters Detective Novel"

Available in paperback and digital formats.